The
Gifting
Programme

SAM NORTH

Minerva

A Minerva Paperback
THE GIFTING PROGRAMME

First published in Great Britain 1992
by Martin Secker & Warburg Ltd
This Minerva edition published 1993
by Mandarin Paperbacks
an imprint of Reed Consumer Books Ltd
Michelin House, 81 Fulham Road, London SW3 6RB
and Auckland, Melbourne, Singapore and Toronto

Copyright © 1992 Sam North

A CIP catalogue record for this title
is available from the British Library
ISBN 0 7493 9875 2

Printed and bound in Great Britain
by Cox & Wyman Ltd, Reading, Berkshire

THE SMALLEST coins are tokens made of base metal and they travel from people's pockets to buy magazines and candy while the shopkeepers nod at their tills and give back change; then maybe a bum gets lucky and drearily watches a paper note fold into his Styrofoam cup; quarry money further and it works via a plastic card that can buy, say, a Trinica fridge, or a gold card which can reach a Platoon auto; then it's buying other money, paying off interest on debt; further up the line it hides, the tellers salting it away behind reinforced glass screens (they're expert with their weights, their handling of monies, counting *exactly*), but these hoarders, banks, are only pockets, more or less full, for the use of other banks or conglomerations of 'funds', who explain themselves in cryptic codes and numbers running across the various US pits, down the Topic screens in London, or in Tokyo, prompting deals that take seconds to complete.

In these arenas, money is itself a product, shifted around in byte-sized lumps and measured relative to whichever commodity, and mesmerising, now, with its mantle of power. Here roost the top players (Mitsubishi, Itoh, Mobil, Mitsui), year by year changing places on the listings. Among them rests the complicated Sayers Corporation, built as if by magic on the eccentricity of its six-foot-four tall Chairman, Ambelin Sayers.

When this elderly man looks at people, they feel privileged, immensely famous in a quick flowering of vanity. Their investment plans belong to him. *Debts* even, are his *assets*.

1

But strangely, money isn't well known to Ambelin. If a child were to ask for enough to buy an ice-cream he would pat his pockets, frown, it would throw him.

This (and other eccentricities) means eveyone knows Ambelin Sayers' name. Among the hectic scheduling of information and entertainment he gets more than a fair share: the press are on to him and the TV networks not only borrow from the press but seek their own rumours; the whole pan-media circus gleans his fame and wealth and they swallow the tiniest tidbit, returning constantly, so the carcass grows thinner and becomes tasteless. They chase Ambelin Sayers because he can sell for them, between the pages of advertisements, or on their screens that jump and glow in people's homes (the pictures sent direct by terrestrial transmission, bounced off satellites, or funnelled via underground cable networks). *Millions* are watching him, but this boils down to enough actual individuals . . .

There are two people, especially, who once knew Ambelin. Now, they watch more closely than usual because he is the innocent victim of a celebrity status show.

Amie Moss, mother of one, partner to none, dressed as always in a long pleated skirt and boots, puts a coin into a small ten-inch screen fixed by a durable wing of dirty plastic to an airport-lounge chair and watches the studio audience rewarding the host of the show by pushing out, extra hard, their embarrassed laughter. She thinks, Ambelin *Sayers*.

The second individual: Buddy Maze, living now for fifty-five ebullient years, rolls indoors, into the shade, playfully holding the remote behind his back until he hears the car's pips – it's alarmed. Now he'll watch some tube. 'Hell, *Ambelin* . . .'

The audience might be anyone, of course, and anywhere in the world. The televisual pinpoint of light scans them the same, so fast you can't *see* how cleverly it runs along the lines and down the screen. TV can open doors and get anything it wants – if not, then it can be made up, and in any case it will be saved and stored forever, in a permanent collision of light and magnets.

Think of anyone and they might be an audience.

There is, for example, a third individual, Wik Slavery, a worrisome New Yorker of thirty-three, who has a connection with Ambelin (but he doesn't know how it happened). He tags the 'on' button and becomes a rating.

The beam of the host's smile rides on electrical energy. No wonder its splendour, incited by the full attention of so many millions.

The show puts up a series of photographs of this ageing eccentric, Ambelin Sayers, all pictures seen before, but the three individuals are watching a deal more closely. They observe the way the old man hangs: like many tall people he appears as though invisibly suspended in gravity rather than rooted by the feet, because his legs, too long, are only following; also they note that his hands are diminutive, that his nose is hooked but his eyes are not in the Greek or Jewish fashion, they're set shallow, focused long, small and black as coal, lying in a puff of flesh, that his grey hair squiffs untidily at the sides but some long strands trek from one side to the other over a mountainous baldness (conscientious vanity, charming because it fails so badly in an otherwise mysteriously successful man).

They listen to a list given of famous disguises he's donned, at various times, to escape his isolation.

The terrifying success of this man.

In one photograph he's angry, looking over his shoulder, pursued by something or someone unknown, here he's giving an oath, his mouth open, a thin arm in the air, the shading of the newspaper ink making him look tired, then he's rumpled and uncomfortable, standing at a picket-line. In some of the pictures

3

he's besieged by microphones: either batteries of them set up to confront him, or they swarm like insects' eyes, after him.

They are candid shots, blown up to scatter the density of print.

In every one he looks unhappy.

The host's voice keeps coming. 'Yup, one guy. Ambelin Sayers. The buck stops here.'

THERE'S THE beginning of a smile on his face.

He is wearing pyjamas, sitting in the aviary of his home, named the Blue House, set in acres along the side of a thin New England lake.

It is dark. His unblinking gaze aims eastwards, watching for the first colouring of dawn.

The snoring rails – shy, flightless birds from Sulawesi – are already sounding in their 'set' of rattan thickets. The earliest songsters.

A peeor joins in; its small body flurries across. As though it were a matter of urgency that it should reach the opposite corner of the aviary! (A sheet of colour is being pulled surprisingly fast up that eastern drop of the sky.)

The wrinkles on Ambelin Sayers' face, lit from the side, stand out: a moulded map of age.

It's not every morning he's here this early to watch his birds, but he needs the cathartic effect of their sound (building to such a clamour). His eyes search for detailed colour of their design; his ears log the different calls . . .

Pleasure.

He is overfull, it is glorious, this emptying of affection, and necessary: he can no longer walk around with it unused.

4

Because there is so much feeling in him today. His heart is a fist tightly holding a secret – he wants to unfold it.

Standing now, he lifts his chin. His lips move. His hands are half curled, arms low but outstretched. He's whispering the words to a Latin *Vesperi*.

At Somerville, emotion stuck to the singer, a boy – such grandeur.

Tonight, when he goes to bed, he will be sure to sleep. He will have time to take up some singing . . . He will have . . .

A young man soft-shoes into the aviary through the glass trap, carrying with him two briefcases. Respectfully eyeing his employer, he moves to an inoffensive position. He *quietly* puts the briefcases down and adopts a waiting stance: weight equally divided between both legs, arms folded. He checks his watch.

He coughs, gently.

He is frightened in his job, although he enjoys sensing its importance: not knowing about status, Ambelin is innocent with his wealth and this makes him vulnerable; he needs an adviser, even, to hire his advisers, and for weeks at a time he's fielded from meeting to meeting like an obscure specimen, inspiring a magical respect.

The Chairman of the Sayers Corporation shouts, 'Can't they all come in their pyjamas? Call 'em up and tell 'em to come in their pyjamas!'

The assistant's hand doesn't quite want to go to the phone. He must judge that this is not a serious suggestion . . . He watches his boss shuffle back and forth. It is part of his job, this reading of Ambelin; he is an interface between the man's genius and the pragmatic demands of the Sayers organisation. Ambelin might forget what he's said or change his mind, or this might be what the assistant defines as a 'ride' – something that his boss determines, that's unwavering.

Ambelin wants the day to run on faster. He's thinking, Three true affections. Their value . . . he was about to define them as being priceless, but that's what you might say about an expensive painting. These affections will be . . . it is impossible . . . friendship is beyond all scale of measurement. Its value is *religious* . . .

A second man comes silently across the lawn, bowed and creaking with age. Winston. Carrying clothes.

The assistant is relieved to see this confident oldster's face as he nods and passes by – now he is saved from having to go too close to Ambelin. He watches in awe as Winston walks over, starts to unbutton Ambelin Sayers' pyjamas and talks to him.

Winston, who has been in charge of the three invitations, says, 'Last day.'

Ambelin's hand comes up and stops him as he reaches the second button. He calls out, 'Tell 'em we're on our way.'

The assistant is spurred – he diplomatically takes up the receiver – but he's still unsure. He's going to delay his reply. He waits, judging the mood . . .

Ambelin Sayers slaps down Winston's hands and refastens the top button. Winston does not attempt to calm him.

The assistant decides to leave his briefcases parked and advances on the knot made by the two older men. High above them the Oahu creeper, invisible, flutters – a sound Ambelin first heard while listening to a tape recording in Hawaii . . .

'Sir, if I could just run through our schedule – we would be a little early.'

Ambelin Sayers begins to move. The assistant takes two paces backwards.

'Sir, it's barely dawn . . .'

A spasm of unstoppable happiness invades Ambelin Sayers. He ignores the assistant and pushes past, lolloping out while struggling to find the words to Byrd's *'Agnus Dei'*, *'qui tollis peccata mundi . . .'*

Winston's given up.

They are never upset by the old tycoon, but he is surprising.

After a pause – to recover, to accept the man again – the assistant prods the phone back to life.

He speaks into the mouthpiece. 'Jack? Chairman'll be with you in just over an hour forty. No. Call 'em all up. Get 'em over there fast. He ain't even stopped to eat.'

THE CITY lights, filaments and gases burning all night thousands of feet up, fight off darkness, so when the shadows evenly, slowly back off it's like a victory, allowing morning to grace the skyscrapers – they glisten, refreshed, ready for a repeated onslaught from those millions scouring a more or less big living.

Woken extra early, they are all waiting, way up there.

Jack Cavendish is Keyman CEO for Ambelin Sayers. He joined the Corporation straight from high school and has been carrying his heavy stomach steadily higher up this building ever since. This is his day.

There are eight others. Faces waiting. An account for each life, plus and minus: he has kids but one's trouble; she has no kids but a famous lover; he has his own money but fools himself with it; she's tough but also too tough. Like salmon desperate for the upstream they've jumped hard enough to get this close to Ambelin.

They stand scattered on the fringes of the room, facing outwards. From the huge Glamouround tinted windows they can look down on the (surprisingly rustic) water tanks on all the surrounding blocks.

Getting called so urgently: a good sign?

Jack notes the increase in deference from his colleagues. Their respect for him has been growing steadily. When, at last year's AGM, one of Ambelin's titles dropped down to him (Chief Executive Officer), it was read as the traditional favouring of a successor and, now that he's about to take over, his colleagues' interest is tangible and serious – no humour attached.

Replaced by fear.

He is about to enjoy a moment of considerable achievement. He can taste success again, despite having been successful for so long. These men and women will be his audience.

They are waiting for a sighting of the red and yellow chopper: when Jack Cavendish spots it he keeps quiet out of modesty. Slowly the others gather towards the north-facing side to watch it fly in. It is, after all, a historic moment and not to be wasted.

Protected from the crashing volume by 'proofed tiling, it seems eerily quiet with this giant machine coming so close, edging over to land directly above, flattening the roof garden on top of the building.

According to a plan previously agreed between them, they take their seats. They each have a way, long practised, for slipping into a state of readiness.

8

But when the Chairman walks in they pre-empt his habitual greeting by standing and applauding, still applauding, despite the fact that he's wearing pyjamas under his overcoat (a bad sign?).

The Chairman stops behind his chair and waits, lifting his lined brow. The skins of many rich men are plastic: buffed by wealth, shiny with self-confidence. Ambelin Sayers, the richest of all, does not look like this. He has a grey pallor. There are good reasons for this, he can choose between several: a virulent but temporary invasion of cancer, the bungling heart muscle (he's seen his heart's septal defects painted in dye on a fluoroscopic screen) – or he could blame insomnia. So he might look like a union leader or a retired basketball player, but not a car salesman, because of his elevation and because his eyes will always give him away. They float, never getting caught, always grazing, showing of a nebulous instinct, rarely coming down from such a height.

Then he's frowning – and his power is more noticeable. He is exasperated because this is good news for him, but bad for them.

They wait; he says nothing.

He's thinking, how close have they come to him, these people he works with? They rise to him like children with more than a hint of personal warmth, but it's coming from round the edges, from the minimal gap in their cuffs, their collars, because they're out to greet his wealth. They want to engage with his position, not with him. Affection has an unmistakable music; he's not heard the keynote struck with anyone since he last went walkabout, aping a poor man through the Midwest, and got hosted by the unknowing Wik Slavery . . .

9

Jack Cavendish misunderstands, he reads Ambelin's silence the wrong way, thinking it's just an emotional moment for the old man who's stepping down after all these years. He takes it on himself to fill the gap by striding smartly round the table to offer a handshake. The Chairman (used to just going along with things, in some ways) accepts the gesture.

Jack Cavendish then performs a ceremony: he moves to the sideboard, gingerly lifts the shrouded cage, transfers it to his other hand and lowers it onto the table in front of the Chairman.

So – silence, with smiles . . .

The Chairman does not lift the shroud. They wait.

Within, the bird stiffens, listening in the dark, its beak parked down in its feathered beard.

The Chairman lifts a curled forefinger and places it against his top lip, as though the prow of his nose has slipped and he is about to hitch it back up his face a couple of notches. Those gathered around him recognise this gesture – it signifies he is working out what to say.

'I cannot accept this gift.'

A heavier silence. There's dread, suddenly, around this table. Another delay? Something in Jack Cavendish crumbles and falls.

'Not that I can't recognise the gesture,' continues the Chairman, 'because I can.'

They notice: he's going into speech-mode. Shoes together at the end of the long legs; hands restful; the beakiness, the authoritarian look cruising at his height.

'But I have no intention of misleading you.'

Ambelin hears himself and he dislikes it, his voice is fake

10

because too many people listen, it's distributed so widely that, to him, it's gotten out of key.

It occurs to Jack Cavendish, he should strike the table (as would a child in tantrum) at this hint of things about to go wrong.

'This gift,' continues the Chairman. He indicates the cage. 'No doubt was made in good faith. But, if you see what I mean, it's already paid for. By me . . .'

He takes the chair in front of him, lifts it an inch, then puts it down again. Now he's mumbling to himself. 'So is it really a gift . . . no. But then . . . no, I can't take it.' He looks around the table, a pain of self-criticism gathering in him.

Still silence.

'See, I could kind of *pretend* that we are friends – we've all been doing that happily enough for years – I *could* – but I can't, not now.'

Jack Cavendish, Keyman CEO, successor to Ambelin Sayers, feels panic. What was this speech? Was there a traitor in the room? So – where would the knife go? Into whose back? He looks around the table. Is he out? She? Get anyone out but him, and the others sorted. Then clear up and make good (himself there).

Ambelin Sayers, still Chairman, isn't, for now, aware of the charged quietness. His attention has moved, he's become fixed on wondering what's in the cage.

He lifts a corner of the shroud . . . it's a bearded wood-partridge or *Dendrortyx barbatus* – and a female.

He waits until after the familiar double skip to his heartbeat and adjusts his breathing. He cups a hand to the back of his neck and purses his lips. A kindly expression invades. That is something – *good gift!*

He already has a male, captured secretly after a recording

was made near Pueblo Rico in Eastern Mexico and he couldn't buy out the owners fast enough. The deforestation is running at a worse pitch, but he owns enough now, around that town, to put these two together, watch some breeding, then return them . . .

Ambelin is haunted by birds. He used to like to hold them in his hand, to sense the warm skin-and-bone energy of these creatures, but now he doesn't want to interfere. He thought of himself as a collector, but the predicament of birds and their shrinking habitats has turned him, like some others, into an aviculturist – a collector with a role. Red siskins, for instance, were first sought for the rare gene which could carry red plumage into canaries and other common cage birds; now aviculturists like himself own pairs only to breed and reintroduce them, non-hybrid, back to protected environments.

He looks at the bearded woodpartridge again. The same back-curled beard feathers. The same angry look all the time. Fierce things! Casting a bright look to each of the assembly he says, 'I can tell you this would have been the best, darn, the best gift I could have had, you've done real well, all of you . . .'

He is carelessly pinching the shroud between his long fingers, sounding bewildered: 'But I can't take it.'

'Sir!' Jack Cavendish comes in an octave too high. He tries again. 'Sir . . . we must walk out of this door with semi-knowledge of the position. Journalists are waiting in Alexander and I have to feed them something of concrete value . . .'

'Soon.'

'Sir, it must be today.'

Ambelin Sayers can ride this now, he needn't listen to talk about deadlines or sales-force motivational structure or just-in-time or anything else they try to bother him with in their

12

sharpening of profits. He could easily sit here and fuss over this bird . . .

'Listen,' he says, then checks the bottom of the cage. Yes, a mixture of sand, wood and bark – someone knows what he's doing.

He's lost track. What was he going to say? He's got more lines than most men on his forehead; they fall into a new place.

'Where was I?'

'Sir,' begins Jack Cavendish.

'This pile is my pile . . .' Ambelin's not sure if he's finishing up on something he's already said, or starting anew. His eyes travel from side to side, taking everyone in – something he learnt in an expensive PR charm school, but he can't do it properly, it doesn't come off, he looks like a drugged animal. He continues, 'I've paid my price for it. My heart's been sick. My soul, also. Both have demanded something of me. I cannot refuse. Last ditch maybe. But it's all there is. I have to do it.'

Jack Cavendish flushes from the neck up. Sweat is pressed from his skin. 'You're Chairman, sir.'

He immediately regrets saying it.

The Chairman's finger goes to his throat and hooks behind the top button to loosen it.

'No, no,' he murmurs. He is talking to himself. 'I'm standing by what I say.'

Ambelin is already half-turned to take his leave when he continues the mumbling but without saying any real words – and wheels back again.

Because he can't just *leave* it.

Making a cooing sound, in recognition, Ambelin picks up the cage.

They watch (in awe) as he negotiates an exit.

Two

A MAP OF the US shows a fat, bowl-like collection of nations filled with interconnected nomenclature, but the routes between people, the thought-paths, silent conversations uninterrupted by technology, imaginative visits which all men and women make (busier and more truthful than phone-lines) are unmarked.

Ambelin's been remembering only three people.

Now he's touched on them via US Mail, hoping to draw them in. The invitations are made from the thinnest fillet of wood possible before it might be defined as paper. A heavy thread of twenty-four-carat gold is crimped onto the edge; the summoning words are embossed in black. There are only three in existence.

The first invitation lies torn into pieces on the floor of a garage in West Virginia.

Amie Moss looks fit for her age partly because she wears long skirts and collared blouses (to hide her neck). She has a prominent mouth area, a slight hint of the ape, she always thinks. Her long hair now has colour in it, 'Rich Ochre'. The rough complexion irks her of course, like she's been leaning into a strong wind for her life's work. She dreads the next phase of ageing, the fifties, which will see her into pension-hood.

14

She is sitting on the plain wooden chair looking down to where she dropped the torn invitation – reluctantly, hoping that it might have disappeared and she might be about to wake up.

In front of her there's a mountain of liquor bottles, all different colours. A spectacular sight, in a way. If they were full, they'd be worth approximately her debt on the house.

She's holding too much in: bitter pride, anger, shame. All this is ballooning in her, preventing her usual common sense. She knows that her face is out of control, possibly ugly. She covers it with her hands, still not used to feeling the skin so old.

'And it's my birthday,' she exclaims out loud. (Forty-nine years *gone*.)

'Mom!' She hears her son call from the house.

She starts to wipe her eyes, then a thought (he might come in) strikes her and she's scraping at the floor, picking up the pieces.

'Mom!' Closer now.

Two bits left. This corner is hard to pick up (her nails are too chewed to be any use). She pushes it along the floor, cursing.

'You in there?' Her son's voice is quiet – right outside.

'Yuh!' she cries, pretending to be surprised. 'Just coming now.'

He doesn't try the door – she relaxes, fractionally.

She's always protected TJ, thrown a fence around him. His big-secret father is outside the wire, along with other damaging things. She's got control of the gate, allowing entrance selectively, but that's possible only up to his age – somehow he's getting out at night.

She's picked up the invitation; now she looks for some-

15

where to hide it . . . Behind the tool bench? No, she'll want to retrieve it in order to ditch it properly, because the invitation mustn't remain in existence. So she slides the roughly torn sections under a piece of curtain resting in the well of an old wheel. She'll burn it later.

'Just coming now, TJ.' She opens the door, but her son is no longer there (being tactful?). She wanders into the house to find him.

The rooms depress her: their new atmosphere of carelessness. How quickly they've come to look lost, left out. Boxes are enclosing her life's pieces, turning them into just so much bric-à-brac.

Her son is waiting, in fact, to remind her of her age with a birthday present (she's always surprised that he's taller, when she's so much older). His brand-new face is impassive as he hands it over.

'*Thank* you.'

She can't stop him from growing his hair that long. It is getting difficult, though, to guess what he's thinking, or what's in his pockets. She used to know; now that she's not allowed, she really wants to find out.

Unwrapping the present, from time to time she stops with a finger under the paper and checks his expression. He is watching the parcel, not her.

Inside she finds a better make of ladies' watch.

She frowns. And gathers herself for moral duty.

'Where'd you get the money to buy this?'

He doesn't answer.

'Huh?'

Instead he waits . . .

Now he is looking at her. He moves his weight from side to

16

side. For some time they consider each other. Then a smile twitches sadly on his face.

'Just a watch, Mom, not permanent heartache.' His voice is broken but not quite male. He turns, rolling on his new Sidewinders.

And she didn't buy him those sneakers.

In order to avoid taking the blame for his behaviour she notices dirt and odds and ends on the way to getting packed up. Where will they go?

She has little Arthur Cinsaretti making offers of salvation, hinting manfully at the depth of his wallet. She has the family lakehouse which her brother won't want to use . . .

Walking quickly, she returns to the garage. For God's sake, she's been driven to break the little chair before now. The abandoned soulless moments she's spent in here. No room for a car in her garage!

She rescues the torn invitation and sits again in the chair. After a while she takes up from where she left off and drops the eight pieces on the floor in front of her, rearranging them to make up the whole.

Maybe she'll go.

THE CHAIRMAN funnels through the corridors of his home. Fantastic objects come by him but he doesn't see. A huge Maverich; a Sloane sculpture; a set of Baccini pastorals; a tenth-century winged altarpiece from Fiorino's destroyed cathedral. He doesn't even glance into rooms of extraordinarily ornate splendour. His gait is stately, although with a loopiness about the knees due to the length of the levers working either side of these over-stressed old joints.

Followed by his dog (a short-haired black and white mongrel called Moon), Ambelin goes outside, heading for the west wing. As he traverses his vast lawn, a sole figure, he tries to add up his loneliness. How would you measure isolation? In terms of year upon year of the stuff, a time-based reckoning? Or with a scale of intensity, like a Richter type of thing they use for earthquakes?

All those people who'd crowd near if they could. It's only the fences stopping them. Even on Lakeside they had to float a barrier across the water to stop both press and public from getting in. The crush of strange faces around him all these years – and every time any one mouth opens he can see it is filled with money.

The Chairman lifts a hand to shade his eyes as he hits a patch of sunshine. He is tiny against the expanse of green lawn. If the helicopter there, seen from above, takes on the proportions of a grasshopper, he's that small as he trawls to the main entrance, talking with Moon. His voice is a worried vibration. But it can be heard.

He slugs it out across the turf.

THE SECOND invitation is in the breast pocket of Mr Wik Slavery. He's standing face-on to the mirror in his therapist's foyer. Given, the mirror is tinted, but even so his looks are good. He has the height necessary to have most girls comfortably under his chin, he has the face, the high-horse expression cultivated by the medium wealthy in New York, he has his physique trimmed of excess and his complexion is tinted twice – once by a sunny hunting expedition and again at the club.

'Smashed mirrors have been known to pick themselves up and reassemble.'

It's a line remembered from an ex-girlfriend who'd been asked what her new lover looked like (he was grateful for that anyway).

He has a straight nose, level brows, eyes wide apart and blue, a finely drawn jaw under thin lips, but most of the handsomeness hangs on the slanted cheekbones (rarely seen in these parts).

If only there had been one event, an adventure or, better, an achievement, that had happened to him, that would have as big an impact on people. His looks influence women, he collects glances, gathers and counts each one as an affirmation of his ability to cut maybe an enviable path through life, but men rule him out as if he weren't one of them. But he is a man. A small anger creases his mood. He is a fine man.

His therapist is a woman. Called in to begin his session, Wik recognises the meanness that always occurs to him at this time: talking is a waste of good money when he can say the same things to himself. To overcome it he pays in advance, writing a cheque immediately.

The therapist encourages the use of humour as a lubricant to help ease her clients towards an understanding of their intra-, inter- and extra-personal anxiety. She's proud of having read the textbooks but then not using them, instead relying on common sense. She's not too much one of the listening variety of therapists, because she has an endless string of questions – answering them is like drawing a tissue from a box: there's another one straightaway ready.

'So Wik,' she begins, 'd'you do what I said?'

'I always do.'

19

'OK, what d'you bring?'

Wik reaches into his inside pocket and withdraws Ambelin Sayers' invitation. He places it on the desk between them.

'Now let's have a look, can I?'

Incredulous, she asks, 'Ambelin Sayers?'

'Seems so.'

'*The* Ambelin Sayers?'

'Yes.'

'D'you know him?'

'Never met him in my life.'

'So why's he inviting you?'

'I don't know. I guess he wants something.'

'Money? You got a lot of shares?'

'I don't have a single idea what he wants.'

Suspiciously, she asks, 'You trying to prove something?' Then she pretends to put it out of her mind. 'OK, it doesn't matter for us, let's concentrate on the job we're doing here. So, pick up the invitation, hold it in your hand.'

Self-conscious, Wik holds it aloft as though showing it to a crowd.

'Now' (she is a relentless woman), 'let me explain something that I think. We all have a kind of a kernel, a nugget of self-worth inside us, real valuable of course, and it is only ourselves, only us, who can take away from that nugget or add to its value. D'you see?'

'I don't all the way agree.' Wik Slavery is beginning to get one of the momentary injections of confidence that he comes here for; something to do with paying her gives him licence.

He adds, 'Someone can say something and it will knock you off your perch whether you like it or not . . .'

'Only if you swallow it. Kind of looks like the outside

world's done it, but it's you, in reality. It's what you listen to. What you choose to believe. So what you brought me today means something . . .'

Wik interrupts: 'It's an invitation, is all.'

'So it is. This invitation. To kick off, the most interesting thing about it is, it's from someone, for Chrissake, you don't even know.'

Wik Slavery's facial tic is disguised as a yawn. It comes on when he feels this muscularity invading him. 'So what?'

'So it's your status again, isn't it, that we looked at before? You're not anxious about yourself inside, but anxious about what others have you billed as, huh? You're hooked on outside opinion? We already did this shrinking-personality thing of yours, we got that clear, well this is a manifestation . . .'

'I think you're reading too much into it.'

'OK, do this thing for me.'

'OK.'

'You're holding the invitation. Now define for me what it does that makes you feel more valuable.'

Wik answers too fast. 'The fact that it's from him to me. From someone as important as him, to me – but why not? Anyone would say the same.'

'Would they?'

Wik replaces the invitation, then picks it up again. That nugget. The worry is that it grows so big so quickly. It is potentially overwhelming. The therapist could hardly advise him to walk around holding this invitation all the time like a comfort blanket. But it's a magic wand. When he replaces it, he dwindles rapidly, feels lonely.

If only his wife hadn't gone. The nugget – maybe there's no

nugget. Nugget? Fucking nugget? What's he thinking about? There's nothing there after all, little happening in this room except rounds of opinion going on, back and forth . . . Maybe she's playing mind-games to earn her fee.

Of course she's playing mind-games to earn her fee. That's her job.

Wik Slavery senses a galloping, a seething . . . what? Hate?

He yawns.

She's talking.

It's panic. It's time for him to win something back.

She's saying, 'Remember this theory, that you have to know yourself before anyone will want to know you . . .'

He tries (after all it's allowed, he's paying her, he's boss), but fails, to interrupt.

On the way out after the session he catches sight of himself in the mirror, but this time his face appears in the bottom left-hand corner of the frame.

The invitation is dented in his hand.

AMBELIN MUST at least try to sleep.

Moon follows him, hung-dog, until they reach his bedroom. The man crosses onto the carpeted surface but his dog stops and sits down. The Chairman turns to check.

'Good girl!'

He adds, 'You know, don'cha, girl?'

Moon sweeps the corridor with her tail. She has no idea why Ambelin gets angry if she goes in here. It doesn't make sense. Part of the puzzle.

He turns down the bed (it's eight foot long to cope with his

22

height). He checks the oxygen, the heart/lung stroker. The defibrillator is on permanent stand-by.

He sits on the bed and takes both slippers off. He can see the open doorway. Moon points her ears, her muscles tense; she nearly stands.

'Stay!'

He checks his watch: twelve noon. He fills a glass with mineralised water. He pulls the pyjama shirt over his head; he will have a fresh one.

The linen sheets have a quality coolness but not even this will suffice, he knows. He lies back on the pillows and takes in a considered draught of air – as though it's medicine.

Then he gets up to draw the blind. Shadows close down to fill the room. Moon, brightly inquisitive in the corridor outside, assumes a new significance, framed by the doorway, splitting up sunlight.

He goes to close the door, leaning on the handle like a parent. Moon backs away and watches regretfully.

A small thread of light is peeping from under the blind. He corrects this and refastens the Velcro.

When he's finished, ready to try for sleep, the Chairman's face is partially obscured by a blindfold the shape of a pair of sunglasses, but first he speaks into the intercom, his voice running with anticipation. 'Winston?'

After a while comes the tinny reply.

Ambelin asks, 'Is Amie Moss coming?'

'Yes.'

He drops back on the pillows.

Other days have ended with Ambelin having won a new hunger, a new potential, almost without trying, because his success is down to him following strands of interest –

suddenly involving – and this curiosity manifests itself more fiercely than in most; he mines it wilfully and with superior intelligence. But as for today, at the end of it he will have . . . how could it be quantified, objectively?

Ambelin's nerves tighten. He can do nothing more. Except worry about how he'll handle the talking. He leaves it at that – he'll just worry.

Outside the room, Moon takes up a final position lying along the bottom of the door.

Inside, the Chairman closes his eyes and sees horses (outlined in red) dancing on the gallops at the top of the hill. He cannot sleep.

THE THIRD invitation is between the Frankfurter fingers of Buddy Maze. He is pointing it at his wife as part of an argument.

'I'm gonna turn it down. No sweat, just a simple thank-you anna fuckin' negative.'

The wreck of his breakfast occupies most of the table. Grits, biscuits and gravy, sausage, country ham, two eggs still-slippery, coffee, toast and jelly, banana, banana milk – all gone. He's still in his dressing gown; his wife is strapped, buttoned up ready to go to work, and still astounded.

'I didn't know you knew *him* for God's sake.'

There are several reasons for Buddy Maze not wanting his wife to enquire too energetically into his past life.

He shrugs. 'I don't much know him; was like all a long time ago. We were buddies f'ra while, the '50s, before he was anything like what he is now.'

'But you gotta go.'

She adds, chastising him, 'Buddy, please . . .'

Buddy Maze looks to one side. A window. People walking past inevitably look in. He is conscious of cutting an interesting figure in this leafy neighbourhood. He dabs the air with the invitation, which causes his stomach to jog under the crisp white slope of the gown. 'I think it's a no-no.' (He wishes they could hear him outside. Maybe he could get this scene going out on the lawn.)

'For Chrissake,' says his wife.

'No, for *your* sake.' He stops chewing to give his wordplay a better chance of doing well.

He's entertaining to look at. Heavy pink lobes decorate his ears. His hair curls, he has bug eyes, he likes cigars. When he pulls smoke into his mouth his cheeks indent, pop out. Then he might squint. Because he works at the ends of his cigars with his teeth there's often a shred of tobacco leaf on his lip. He doesn't believe anything or anyone, least of all himself. Only to his appetite is he straight.

'Buddy . . .' (his wife's hips are just too big for that costume, too fucking big by miles), 'Buddy,' she continues, 'you have to think of yourself sometimes, you know? You bin trackin' ads 'n' all for I don't know how many . . . days, like lookin' for somethin' to get a hold of to get your job prospects up and runnin'? Now this guy might just have an answer. So don' worry about me. Just stop worryin' about *me.*'

She looks like a piece of airport baggage, he thinks – rich and lumpy. Then he reminds himself that if she does look like a suitcase, it's packed with cash.

'Honey,' he says seriously, 'you can't treat a mastectomy like the fuckin' hairdresser.'

25

'I will be all right. Hell, we're tough enough folk. Go through more 'n 'at if we had to. Go on with it, Buddy. I'm not goin' to re-schedule and I'm not goin' to let you stay here 'n' look after me.'

'OK OK.'

His wife smiles.

Buddy adds, 'But I'm comin' straight fuckin' back.'

Now she's stepping towards him. He has to put up with it, as so often before. She says in her baby voice, 'You're my man, you know that? You are.'

'OK.'

'My man.'

Her face distresses him. As he folds her over the hummocky contour of his stomach he sighs with relief because it's gone past. Her goitre is locked onto his shoulder. He hears the car keys grating in her hand.

So now he closes his eyes and allows a small breath to sound through his nose. She's reading it, because she draws back, looks him in the eye.

'What's wrong, honey?'

'Nothin'.'

'Honey, I know you better 'n that. What's wrong?'

'No no. Go to work. You'll be late.' He adjusts the level of nervous irritation: up just a notch on the volume. His hands flutter. 'I'll be OK.'

'I know what it is.' She is deadpan serious. 'I thought you were *OK* after we flew to Trinidad.'

He stares (asking himself, Is this vulnerable enough?).

She knows why his face is all stony. She's sure now.

'It is that, ain't it?'

'Awwww . . . I'm a fuckin' shit you know? A fuckin' shit shit shit.'

26

'No you're not.'

'*I am!* To be more worried, here, in the guts, about flyin' in an airplane than about my wife's mastectomy? How's that for shit? Shitty enough? Satan would hate him-fuckin'-self for that.'

'Don't swear, honey, it's ugly.'

'I'm sorry. You're right, it's ugly. I'm sorry.'

She's calling his swearing ugly? Look at her, the fat purse, who's talking about ugly?

She says, 'Listen. You can take the Merc, drive up there . . .'

'No, I'm gonna try . . .'

'Look, I'm late for work now. As far as I'm concerned you're taykin' the Merc and drivin'. I'll plan for that, OK?' She picks up equipment: a leather bag, papers. She's feeling good and he can squeeze the generosity out with his looks. He stands with his hands on his hips, giving her his famous perplexed expression. He knows his hair is tousled up.

She plants a kiss, two fifties, and she's gone.

Ten minutes for safety; a check that she's not left anything behind; then he picks up the phone and dials.

When the receiver is lifted at the other end he speaks softly, secretly, to a woman in much better shape.

'We got the Merc and two days, two nights. How 'bout that?' He listens for a while.

Then he interrupts, 'What you fuckin' wearin', baby?' A smile moves the fat on his cheeks. 'OK, I'll wait.'

A pause – she comes back on the line.

'Hell! Fuckin' bitch!' He moans and slips a hand under his gown.

'Tell me. Yeah?'

'What sort of top?

27

'Colour?' He's beginning to get going. He grips the phone harder, rejoicing in the lunge of feeling in his groin. After forty years of sex it gets difficult to find anything much that will work. He orders, 'Pull one strap down. Is it down? The other. Yeah! Look down at your tits. Are they both out there? Big enough for me? Are they round and firm? Are they out there? Are they shoutin' for me?'

This is aural sex. He'll come.

IF THE THREE things that make a hotel successful are location, location and location, the Dewdrop Inn was always going to boom: it is five miles from Ambelin Sayers' key home. There's been a price: every so often it is racked with scandal – bugging devices, cash drop-offs, mob fights, blackmail attempts, kidnap, coercion, attempted fraud, the Defense Suppliers Registration Number scandal, S and L of course, one call-girl got famous for a while and there were the unforgettable exploits of the Sayers Security baseball team (Capt. Vincent Aldabo) – all these real-world events surrounded Ambelin Sayers but somehow never touched him, only got as far as the hotel and the people staying there.

The General Manager's back has an extra stiffness because he is waiting for secrets to explode (inevitably this means a flashbulb will pop or a sungun will get pointed in his face).

Now all three invitees have checked in. None of them is known to any of the others.

Ambelin sits in the limo, watching the Dewdrop Inn from across the highway. He is dressed in celebration clothes: blue silk shirt, a summer-weight linen suit. Although, like others among the rich, he owns the necessary all-over badge of quality clothes, as soon as they're off the hanger and on his back they look wrong, like a fashion experiment gone awry during a marketing push on the over-sixties: his used-up body doesn't match the pristine cut and hang of the cloth. Somewhere along the way, he's lost his tie.

It was never part of the scheme for him to have come down here, but up at the Blue House he was waiting (he hated it), just doling out the moments, and they dawdled so meanly, those beats of time, when watched closely.

Also, despite the kicking-in of his recent optimism he wasn't able to let go of a worry: his memory. Most of his life's bloom has been down to a magical instinct for future change, but maybe he's bad at the past, at memory, perhaps tyrannised by his *imagination* of it. If he's made it all up in his head?

Running on a new track, he's now anxious to see if they do all have the same memories of him as he has of them.

Moon is sitting up on the leather, panting heavily, eyes wide, passing concerned sideways looks, making sure he's still there. She hasn't seen these clothes on him. Sometimes Ambelin makes a mistake and leaves her in the limo. She wants to be let in on whatever's going on, not that she ever gets tired of trying to guess.

(Incomprehensibly, the door closes on her.)

Ambelin frightens himself with this thought: that he might die before he sees them. Those veins plucked like worms from his legs, can they hold up in his sternum? Because for Ambelin, at this fateful time, every pace is a step closer to renewal.

When his charismatic figure enters the lobby of the

Dewdrop Inn there's a marked effect on the staff, although he is unaware of it. The shouts of the old negro porter are stilled. People stand and watch, as though there's been an accident. The GM looks busy with a pen and an inside pocket. Of course he's always worried now that he might have to catch the old man from falling, like before . . . It was a strange thrill hanging onto such a bag of bones and knowing the power and wealth at the tips of those fingers, such whitened fingers . . . His concern is always to bounce any trouble, to funnel it out to the other side of the door by waving his hands and using his quiet voice.

Ambelin is tall enough to see over people's heads. His small eyes are fresh with resolve.

He's got the room numbers.

The lurch given him by the elevator coincides with his sense of anticipation. He must hold on.

He tracks the numbers.

Wik Slavery is napping in a darkened suite 702 when he hears the knock. Annoyed, he turns the switch on the bedside light and prepares to meet a bellhop with a luggage problem, or room service – something troublesome anyway, but it's a tall figure, richly dressed, standing there outside the door and staring at him, an old face . . . and famous . . .

Nothing said.

Wik stiffens. It's Ambelin Sayers. Why's he come down here, ahead of the invitation? Is this the time everyone expects, when you have to deal with the one bit of trouble that life's bound to throw at you when you're least expecting it?

There's something wrong. Not just the man's overly intense stare, but the way his build is awry with age – the plate of his hips is set badly, the legs are skewed . . . he looks ill.

'D'you remember me?'

'You're Ambelin Sayers . . .'

'But d'you remember where we met before?'

Wik Slavery frowns and tucks (suddenly loose) fingers away in the cord of his gown.

'Met *before*? No . . . I'm sorry?'

Worry creases Ambelin's face. He gives the clues quickly – success must be held onto else it will slip away.

'A certain pick-up? Five years ago?'

Wik is startled. Is it a joke? Because yes, he knows, he knows . . .

'Hang on, say, are you who I think you are? You are the guy . . . aren't you the guy. . .?'

Ambelin is relieved. Clipping his fingers round the edge of the doorframe, he looms over the shorter man. He announces: 'It is me.'

He enjoys Wik Slavery's surprise.

Wik is suffering. Why has he been tracked down? 'You . . .'

'Me!'

'God, is that . . .'

'Ambelin Sayers, pleased to see you again.'

'That . . . that was you? Ambelin Sayers? In my pick-up?'

Ambelin leans forward, beaming like a trickster conjuring for a small child. 'That's right, it was.'

Wik is geeing his brain along, trying to hit on more memories. How was it . . . the tall stick of a figure in the road, the snow on the shoulders of his coat, his face stooping in through the side window of the pick-up, the near silence as they travelled, the food in the guy's beard . . .

'If I'd known, I . . .'

Ambelin slips past Wik into the underlit interior of the suite

31

and is standing there like an antique wraith. Wik felt the push against his shoulder . . . was that . . . did he do something wrong back then? Would he be punished for anything here?

Ambelin says, 'That was one of my, kinda, *experimental* times, what you saw.' He has a nerve nagging in the corner of his eye – he's learnt to recognise it as a sign of over-excitement. He wants to reach out and touch Wik Slavery; instead he shakes his head, smiles and waves a fist at him in a dramatic sign. 'A plain, friendly young stud, Wik Slavery, you were, and an ordinary enough bloke, but the only darn person to show me kindness without being asked – see? That's why I'm here.'

Wik Slavery is confused; it's like he's won a prize without entering for any competition – which is *cheating*, after all, so he's uncomfortable. It's turning into bad news, this invitation – there's been a trick played on him and he can't yet see why.

'Sorry for barging in,' begins Ambelin, but then he stops himself, shuts up that avenue of apology. He's having difficulty controlling his mood, slipping between shyness and excitement, muddled . . .

He must reach, get to why he's here.

So he comes out with what sounds like an emergency: 'I had to come and find out if you actually remember. What your memories are. Do you have memories of me?'

But there's silence.

He asks again, 'D'you have any memories?'

The question hangs – seriously.

Wik Slavery is flustered; he's going to have to speak. Ambelin is expecting an answer.

Ambelin has no fond smile now; he looks stricken. 'If you don't remember at all . . .'

Wik Slavery feels compelled to clear his throat and begin. Instinctively he goes very cautiously.

'I remember . . . I remember you, yeah, very well. Often I think about it.'

'What d'you think, when you . . .' Ambelin makes loops in the air with his hand, trying to encourage the other man.

Wik replies, 'The whole thing, all of it, no, most of it anyways, the best bits I guess. Picking you up – the snow all on your shoulders, looked real cold. Was in Wyoming . . .'

'Montana.'

Ambelin's hand has stopped, the long, knuckly fingers held to a point, as though retaining a moment too delicate for stronger handling; Wik catches a look of hurt from him.

Wik can't remember, rightly, but he feels bound to carry on.

'Montana. On the way to Montana . . . My mom was alive back in those days. But you weren't like . . . were you down on your luck, or what?'

'No, an experiment, like I said. Done seriously, though, I wasn't playing. I was starving, for real!'

'You looked almost ready to eat anything.'

'I could have eaten a horse.'

'I gave you cigarettes . . .'

'You gave me everything. I still recall the first meal we had. Maybe you do too?'

Wik Slavery eases his posture nervously. 'The meal?'

'Yeah, what was it, what did we eat? D'you remember?'

'Was it . . . Did we get home by then? Was it the soup?'

Ambelin waits. 'Soup?' he asks. 'You sure it was the soup?'

As always when he is on the defensive, Wik feels his nerves whip tight and he yawns.

Ambelin is quick to apologise: 'Christ . . . I'm sorry, you're

33

tired an' all after the journey, and trying to take a nap, and here I am . . . Of course, we can talk later.'

But he can't help smiling and asking, suddenly, framed by the doorway, 'What sort of pick-up d'you drive, that day?'

'A Conway Cruiser.'

Ambelin brightens. 'That's right . . . You lent it me, remember, I used to drive over to that place?'

'You drove it?'

'That's right, that's . . . You lent it me. Often I took myself off over to that bar, with my foot on the gas, bouncing your pick-up all round the place I used to, and you never gave any complaint!'

'Right . . .'

Ambelin wants to finish off with an embrace but he's never done that because he's been too tall, always. He's backing away, unaccountably shy, muttering and scanning the floor like when he was a child and had told small fibs to grace himself more favourably in some adult's eye.

When he's gone, Wik is left, churned up.

So Ambelin (hauling his frame along a warren of corridors on the third floor) recognises the first click of a successful plan. Wik Slavery needed a little prompting and was plainly startled, but that was to be expected. The fact is he *remembered*.

Ambelin imagines music: he would have his favourite piece, with himself singing live to an enraptured crowd, accompanied by a light percussion and some strings. He thumps his rib-cage with the heel of his hand. It feels tight in there.

He shouldn't have left Moon in the limo, Moon should be scouting ahead of him here . . .

The doors all look the same, except for the changing

34

numbers, like a lottery – who are behind the faceless panels? Different people, others, but he, Ambelin, has the code, the right numbers, his people.

304.

Buddy Maze, when he hears the knock, is expecting a free gift, this being the kind of luxury joint where you get a complimentary something or other coming at you every time you open a closet or lift a toilet seat.

When he opens the door he visibly jumps but uses it to good effect. 'Ambelin, fucking Ambelin! My old buddy!' He has a hand held out ready for shaking.

Ambelin takes it, but he is unsure.

Buddy holds on. It's a much longer handshake than he's ever given. 'This is my wife,' he lies (easily), pointing, but the girl has sensibly trotted into the bathroom. 'She's kinda shy,' he explains.

Buddy's beginning to worry about Ambelin's lack of response.

He tries again: 'Fuckin' Jesus, *look* at you. Thirty-odd years ago and it sure as hell looks like it, on us, don' it?'

Ambelin searches Buddy Maze's face, frowning, breathing heavily. He says, 'It is you . . .?'

'Sure! You made more money but I put on more weight! Hell! How are you?'

A smile crawls across Ambelin's face, getting broader. 'My friend,' he says.

'Sure!'

A bead of spit swings from Ambelin's mouth and then grips on his chin.

He shuffles closer and focuses. 'Buddy Maze.'

'That's right, Buddy Maze.'

'1961 LA . . .'

'We were twisted wrecks, huh?'

It's an electrifying thing, Ambelin's grin. He shakes his head in disbelief and begins to ask, 'D'you know you and me were . . .' but then he pulls himself up. 'Christ, this is doing me in, you know.' He can sense his mood like a loose weight sliding in him, strangely enough bringing him closer to behaving in the manner of those years, when, even though forty years old, he was into playing mind-games like a teenager.

He sits in the comfy and sighs through pursed lips. His eyebrows pop.

But he's on track and can't swerve from asking, 'Buddy, I came here, I don't know, I need to be sure of just one thing, that this isn't the disintegration of an old, well, nearly-old man, alone, who by going on repeating . . . re-running memories, hauling them out you know, underplaying them, overplaying them, in my head, you understand, like in my private movie theatre – but maybe I so often just a bit mistook things about you, and the others, as to have changed the scenes, changed the actual people somewhat?' He suddenly looks haggard, thinking about this possibility.

Buddy begins to play up in front of this important man. His voice echoes in the huge suite.

'Hell, I dunno about that, Ambelin, but I tell you I ain't forgotten. '61 LA was a real special time. I remember all that stuff, in those cars of ours, runnin' the tunnels at a hundred just for the blast, drivin' naked on the bridge, spendin' your money, and the stuff we carried! Hell, we'd have poisoned the whole town if we'd fallen in the drinking water . . .'

'The insults business, remember that, when we tried selling insults? And the dares, d'you remember the dares?'

'Hardly as if I could forget! You still owe me your first-born goddam darn son.' Buddy mocks outrage. 'D'you ever get one?'

'No, I never did . . .'

Buddy instinctively veers from under the cloud of sadness that's hovering. 'Christ, why did we do some of that stuff? We were idiots! Remember drinkin' together that night, 'bout the time we were snuffling all that ether, right, 'n' we set up that newspaper dare, weren't it? Can we think of a way to get into *NationHood* magazine within a coupla weeks? Preferably the front page? Had to do something, both of us, then. There was some fuckin' prize as usual, there was always some fuckin' prize . . .?'

Ambelin points a finger at Buddy. 'What was the prize that time? What was it?'

'A boat,' replies Buddy Maze; 'you'd picked up that big red motherfucker boat someplace. Christ, you got through tons of po-ssessions that's for sure, you used 'em up like hankies . . .'

Ambelin dabs the finger again – 'What was it we thought we'd do?'

'Nuns. Weren't it? Somethin' to do with nuns.'

'What though?'

Buddy fires off, 'I remember it had to do with rapin' and stranglin' a whole bunch of 'em.'

Ambelin opens his mouth and makes a primitive noise – signalling excitement.

'And we did it!' continues Buddy Maze. 'Not like that of course, but we fuckin' got into the mag, didn't we?' He half turns in a pretence at addressing non-existent others, waving a thumb at Ambelin. 'Him, the schmuck, goes and has a smartass idea. Buys an ad? Just his name. Ambelin Sayers.

37

Cost him a few bucks but he was rich as buffalo shit even back then in '61! Me, me, I was a fuckin' dumb animal . . .'

'You know, animals aren't dumb, animals aren't dumb at all.'

'Hey, absolutely not. No . . . but I was! First I called *NationHood* magazine and told 'em I had proof Kennedy was a fuckin' queen. Guess what they said? They said they knew already! Fuckin' jokers. Next I thought of killin' *myself* by inhaling, ingesting an' injecting enough fuckin' narcotics to turn myself into a human bomb, but I figured I'd get caught and go to jail – no way, not even for that amount of fun. So what d'I do?'

Buddy Maze is wrinkled with mirth.

'I can't believe I fuckin' did this. I went to the Mayor's ceremony and I grabbed his wife's tits, remember? I grabbed the fuckin' Mayor's wife's tits and not only that I held onto them. I hung on until the photographer got a picture. Her cones almost came off in my hands I tell you, the fuckers darn near popped then and there!'

'We split the boat.'

'But you trashed it, you trashed it during that mescal jaunt, we got fined – we both fuckin' lost money!'

Ambelin Sayers swears. 'Christ, Christ . . .'

They stare at each other.

Eyes closed, perhaps Ambelin might die in his chair like an ordinary old man. To hear his friend so grandly run the same stories is like magic and in one unravelling stroke conclusively proves the truth of those times, because in the most deserted edge of his isolation he suspected himself of having invented a friend, like a kid left alone after school.

But he's a driven man, he has to catch Amie Moss.

38

Under the brutally hard lights in the restrooms on the second floor of the Dewdrop Inn, Ambelin Sayers begins to laugh. His hair is skewed out of place and he's here to smooth it down, ready for his first meeting with Amie in sixteen-odd years. He moves erratically. He is dog-and-bone happy.

But she's not in her room.

When the GM spots Ambelin trotting across the lobby he and his assistant move like cutting horses, shepherding him towards the front desk, quartering off potential trouble. The lobby music is wrong now, it sounds dangerous.

'Mr Sayers, sir . . .'

'Where is she?'

'If you tell me who you're looking for, Mr Sayers, we . . .'

Ambelin interrupts, 'Amie Moss.'

'Just one minute . . .' The receptionist is tripping on her words. Her Bic flies wildly down the desk; she makes a move for it, then realises she's still talking: 'Ms Moss just this minute checked out, sir. We called a car for her.'

Ambelin is on his way already. The GM makes an emphatic but discreet gesture with his finger to send the AM off in pursuit while he rests nonchalantly against the desk, watching the hurry in the entrance hall.

Outside, Ambelin sees her.

His first thought: she's standing just as straight as before, but heavier.

He recalls the way her hands fluttered and settled only reluctantly. Most often, her casual touching of him was a pat on his high shoulder or a wipe of his forearm, except in love, when she hauled on him as though to save her life.

Even with this new heaviness he can enjoy the former straightness of her posture, but for the way her neck angles

39

overly forward, just a touch like before, giving her (especially when it's a sideways look like now) the appearance of a kindly humanoid from another planet.

A reminiscence: the phone on his knees, trawling through long conversations, delightedly gleaning her humour, sitting late in the night and revelling in not having to care for the charges notching up, each escalation audible, in the silences, as a brief thrumming on the line – such silences, even, were valuable for sensing her youth come at him and quicken the constant message (from her to him): Liven up; be glad.

She meets his gaze evenly.

He has to walk several paces before he can reach her. He wants to take her in his arms but doesn't know . . . how did he do it before?

Her presence, her attention on him. This is exactly the thing. All mood drops away; he feels anxiety drop off in layers. If he stays near like this he'll grow a new skin.

She's pretending not to notice the noises coming from him, noises of someone with a cold: coughing, difficult breathing.

Ambelin Sayers, Chairman of the Sayers Corporation, wishes to hide his face.

He mumbles, 'Amie . . .'

She's curious – but she knows him, she's not going to get taken in.

Ambelin's shoulders droop. He nods to himself, looking down at his shirt-front, murmuring something. He claps the heel of his hand against his breast-bone.

'Ambelin,' she says, sensibly. 'What are you doing, we're meant to be meeting for this big-deal party of yours up at Blue?'

'I s'pose,' he says, slowly, 'I was in a hurry.'

'Hurry?'

She used to have this way of listening to his heaviest woes as they spilled from him: she'd hold his hand and pass her thumb back and forth over the same spot, going on until his nerves would up and run and he could believe she was burning a hole in his skin. Then it could get difficult, to disengage inoffensively, not to snatch his hand back. When he'd succeeded he used to sit on his hand and secretly rub away the irritation. Meanwhile she'd have been fixing him with her concern.

He says, 'There's something I got myself worked up over.'

He pauses.

'What I want to know . . .'

He stops again and lifts a forefinger to his nose.

A wave of sympathy overthrows Amie. Before she has time to stop herself, she puts a hand to the side of his face.

Ambelin Sayers grins – now he is looking forward to her testimony with a decent pleasure. Right here, after all these years, after all the effort, stooped and old as he is, he's bursting with the most savoury success ever: a chance to turn the clock back and defy a long-held regret.

'Amie! Always that deadpan face . . .'

And there's Wik and Buddy in their rooms in the Dewdrop Inn behind him, both . . .

Amie asks, 'What?'

'I just love the memory of you.'

He adds, 'Do you . . .?'

She is confused. 'What?'

'D'you remember me?'

'Of course, idiot.'

'What though? Go on, don't get shy!' He waves at the AM, the other guests (some, recognising him, dawdle to catch more time in his presence), the drivers and hangers-on standing here round the drop-off point, pretending not to watch.

Ambelin says, 'See, you are still my best friend.'

Amie has to talk softly, with everyone looking (she remembers it was like this). 'I – I don't think I've been much of a friend all these years. I've not seen or spoken to you, not since I was thirty-two, you fifty-three. Seventeen years.'

'But there's that trust that exists, ain't there, that lives always between friends.' Ambelin waves one hand from side to side, clearing away her objection.

'I don't know,' murmurs Amie, 'I don't all the way agree. I'm entirely pleased to see you, I am, but I suppose I think friends should be there. Trust seems lazy to me.'

Ambelin is puzzled. He comes up closer, his breath still puffing a little, and examines her, trying to understand.

'You must remember *us* . . .'

She is calm and rational – feels herself behaving in a likeable way. She's not trying to deflate him.

She repeats, 'I remember you, course I do. Not that we knew each other for very long, and it was a fair old time ago . . . In fact I seem to remember but – God this is going to sound kind of a teensy bit ridiculous – but I think you disappeared owing me some money . . .'

A coldness slides in Ambelin's insides.

Amie Moss is struck with the idea of this, its preposterousness amuses her. She begins to smile. She looks around her at the splendid wealth of the hotel, of his clothes – and it was a first-class ticket to New York and then from there by *helicopter*

. . . Her smallest, most friendly laugh escapes her.

Bewilderment is blocking off Ambelin's reasonable thoughts but he's still ready to have it all cleared up by her, rendered harmless, a mistake.

'I owe you money?'

Everyone – the driver, the guests, the liveried doormen, the single photographer who's got wind and turned up – they're all waiting for her, it seems.

Then she says, 'Well, yes, a tiny amount, it didn't matter a bit . . .'

Ambelin feels the numbness within him tear.

He says, 'I can do insults too.'

He adds, 'You . . .'

Even though it's getting towards dusk, Amie puts her dark glasses on.

Ambelin continues, 'You . . .'

She watches tears gild his eyes and remembers that she should now walk off, fast. Ambelin goes after; they follow the sweep of the tarmac round towards the highway. He shouts, 'For Christ's sake!' He has his fists in his pockets.

When they get to the road she starts running to get to the hotel's back entrance. There's no sidewalk – she's among the oncoming cars. She hasn't run like this for years. Her breasts are jumping uncomfortably. It occurs to her that this is what she has always been doing, metaphorically speaking – deliberately running before she needs to, never turning to fight for anything, scared of losing what might be good . . .

His shout is still pursuing her. She veers to the left, away from the road, gaining the side lawns of the hotel. Out of the corner of her eye she senses his track change. He's going to head her off.

43

She's lost her glasses.

At the rear, the hotel car park is a formless grey. The helicopter is lit from within like a station of safety – she makes for it, resenting the damp from the lawn in her flat shoes.

An accident with garden furniture? That's the sound. She sees Ambelin, briefly, as he falls.

By the time she reaches the helicopter, however, he is not far behind. She slams the perspex door, watching his baldness appear beneath her. She sees blood falling from one of his hands.

Breathless herself, she can't hear what he's saying. His mouth moves, disturbing her with its soundlessness. After a while she chooses not even to look at him.

Ambelin turns and makes for indoors.

Amie, still feeling like she's trying to breathe through lungs half full of cigarette tar, is left with the pilot. Although shocked, she remains reasonably calm because she has the advantage of bad things having happened to her before. She might have expected this, with her luck.

She looks at the pilot, who is embarrassed.

Steadying her breathing, she says, half to herself, 'I've never seen anyone . . . in such a state . . . Is he . . .? No . . . he's not all right.'

She can see Ambelin dwindling, a silhouette against the bright red and yellow roadside sign proclaiming the Dewdrop Inn.

Once he's put a certain distance between himself and the helicopter, Ambelin stops and bows his heart closer to the ground. It's racing and skidding wildly. He's pumping air like an old engine. Those transplanted veins – he can expect them to break off, or find new routes under the pressure. Blood

44

knocks uncomfortably hard in his head. He cannot think about what has happened. Doors have to be shut sometimes. Steel doors slammed hard and fast, never to be opened again.

He gets to his feet and walks on, thinking about . . . what shall he think about, quick, anything else . . .

Money. He will think about money, what it's done to him and how it's done it. Money's methods, its ways, its bad habits.

Hard cash, they call it hard . . .!

He keeps walking.

But it's soft, his wealth is; he's been floating, an orphan, myopic, unhungry, yet still so hungry, in a cloud of money, orphaned from real . . . orphaned from any possible . . .

Moon is pleased to see him.

AMBELIN'S PRIVACY – almost anything about it – is saleable. Like they were prospecting for a sight of a rare species, the press used to gather on the small triangle of land that Ambelin could never purchase on the opposite shore of the lake, huddle and point their lenses. Security chief Vincent Aldabo organised the floating of the twenty-foot-high screen (tinted grey-blue, camouflaging it as far as possible in the colour of the water and the sky) to thwart them. Now they have walkie-talkies and wait by both the Lakeside and Driveside gates, hanging out, more or less of them, with their survival kits, their highly tuned attitudes, maintaining surveillance, dogged, worrying for the next scoop, but the scoop's happening, if only they could see and hear through the mile and a half

45

of darkened, afforested parkland and then some dozen walls.

In the dining room of his key home, Ambelin is a little drunk. This rare inebriation doesn't detract from his dignity; rather the opposite, because his gullibility is more evident.

The table is broken down to its smallest component, but still it's too much, just for the three of them. All eight candelabras have been painstakingly lit for the occasion. Music adds a grandness, with the voice of the Japanese tenor Mihoto singing the story of a fisherman struck by blindness as a punishment.

Moon is standing square, her front feet splayed on the polished floor, looking at Ambelin. She's trying to copy his mood but it's been difficult to follow. Her tail drifts idly from side to side. These are events outside of routine.

During this meal, with all this talking, Ambelin's temper is veering from happy to sad and back. It's difficult to forget that there had been four places laid here earlier in the day; Amie's setting has been cleared and the balance is now wrong: whereas before there were two each side of the table, now his position has been centred, and there's no one next to him.

He gets to his feet and a thrill courses through him, so strong a sensation that he strikes out too wildly with his introductory gesture and his shoulder twinges; an immediate hurt starts up.

His eyebrows pop upwards, making discs of the puffs of flesh in which his eyes are buried – he looks owlish.

Wik Slavery and Buddy Maze are watching.

He feels choked and silver dots float in front of him, for some reason. His fresh suit is streaked with cream of spinach. He (unnecessarily) taps his glass with a cheese knife. The lines on his face all move at once.

46

'Now . . . I expect you're all wondering? Why I went to such lengths to track you down?'

He pushes his index finger under his nose, then releases the gesture. It's going to seem like a confession now. He blinks his small black eyes and shakes his head.

'It's simple. You are friends of mine . . .'

No, it's a plea.

'My only friends. You can't know just how difficult that is to say . . .'

He's struggling with an unwanted pocket of air that's found the wrong way down his throat.

'I never said that before. I'm gonna to say it again: you are *friends of mine*! There . . .' He sniffs heavily and lifts his head, watching the words fly round the room.

He moves uncertainly.

'I haven't got time . . .' he begins.

He swings back, talking louder still. 'I'm half dead with this goddam . . . wakefulness, it's a matter of urgency.'

Like a tall building in the teeth of a storm, he holds more or less steady.

'I got all this house and all . . .' (he waves at the room) 'and more, two, three more of these. I own not just companies but whole industries, not just country houses, but countries!'

This annoys him: whenever he speaks he can hear multiple echoes. His speechwriter, his media voices (when TV takes opinion on the economy or on industrial relations or on the marketplace), the intonation of the PR woman (Leslie something), his Press Secretary – these are the people who control his appearance and the delivery of him to the various (what they call) 'audiences'. All of whom, because he is weak, clearly have too much effect: where is his own voice? He only hears it

47

inside his head. Or in the lowest whisper. Or in others'
singing.

'Now . . . This isn't me trying to buy friends. It's me trying
to get close by me the only people who've been real friends.'

Buddy is uncertain but he thinks he smells profit, maybe
he's going to come out of this with something, a parcel of
sorts, an object or a favour . . . 'Real friends, you're not jokin'
Ambelin,' he says, 'you're not fuckin' jokin'.'

'I know about buying. I think I've had just about everything
bought for me in my time.' Ambelin points at the ground.
'Earth . . .' He swivels clumsily and gesticulates at the cupped
ceiling. 'Air! Oceans of water. The fires – the fires of I don't
know how many factories burn for me. But real people, or the
reality of people . . .?'

He continues, 'Money's always in the way. It gets to the
smiles of men and women . . .'

He gasps and stops himself, his mouth working to recover
optimism.

'So, d'you see . . . I hoarded moments, saved from time
spent with . . . with . . . both of you guys!'

Buckling his knees and pushing himself straight again as
though trying to take off, he exclaims, 'I guarded those
moments, kept 'em secret, in fear that if I told . . . anyone! . . .
the memories will belong to someone else. Now, I don't want
this any more . . .'

He waves at his wealth.

'I want – no – I *need*. To give it away.'

Buddy feels a ballooning of interest. Yet he maintains
composure: he looks serious and considerate, somehow
managing to behave as though this happened most days.

Wik Slavery is weakened by any kindness done to him. He

can give happily, but if he receives, affection or just generosity, a rogue vibration of insincerity is set up in him; he feels responsible, in debt to that person, and his personality shivers and falls into that mess of panic above which he lives, suspended.

'I'm being quite selfish about it,' continues Ambelin Sayers; 'it's to save my skin . . . There's nothin' wrong,' he gesticulates again, violently, grandly, and leaves his hand outstretched, 'with all this, but there is something wrong with me. I want out. Not because I'm tired, but because I want to *be* tired, to be properly, easily, ordinarily tired, like an animal that's eaten . . . See, I've no children.'

Silence.

'So it's yours, an equal third – an equal half each, because you are real friends, not ever bought.'

Ambelin adds, 'I mean what I say.'

He is forced to continue, trying to make more fun out of it, in view of the fact they're not answering. 'An' this will be for both of you an opening of a new account, see, already listed with assets, with surplus; almost infinite monies divided in half is still almost infinite. Huh? Divided equally, a fair portion each. How about that?'

'Hell, Ambelin!' Buddy is shocked. Hotness flushes down his arms and he gapes in amazement. 'Fuck, somebody wake me up.' In his imagination some rich treasures are sliding past: fast cars, houses, women, food, serious gambling, quality narcotics, more women, the most antique alcohols, a quadruple-size bathtub, servants, quality clothes, more food and more women . . .

Wik Slavery is lost. A sweat has broken from his forehead. His training (Thursdays) in cognitive therapy tells him not to

49

think too much but instead to hang onto technique: find something else to worry about, however small. So he checks for blemishes in the decoration of the walls and ceilings, and when that fails to work he tries to count the errors of taste in the arrangement of objects – but he can find none. 'Well,' he says, and clears his throat.

Ambelin says, 'I have this whole pack of lawyers following me, doing business. I've told them: split it, give. So they're worrying like wolves over the paperwork, and all my money, all my things, can be halved and handed over, if we do something called a gifting programme.'

He looks down at them sitting in their places, the arrangement of cutlery and glasses disassembled after the meal.

He adds, smiling, his eyebrows raised high, 'It makes us, like, a family?'

Three

ELECTRIC LIGHT issues from a single bulkhead fixture in the yard, silvering the rain as it falls through from the dark, heavy and silent, apparently marshalled in straight lines, but this is effected by the light.

When Ambelin goes into the stables the downpour sounds louder; it's driving down seemingly harder to battle against the tiled roof.

His head and shoulders soaked, he stands in the alley that runs between the matching sets of four stables. The floor under his feet cambers gently towards the drainage gully to one side, setting his ankles only slightly off balance, but, like a fault in the bottom-most setting of any structure, the error is magnified by height and age.

Stuck in darkness until he reaches the repeatedly inconvenient location of the light switch, Ambelin positions himself by counting the uprights which support the front hoarding of the stables, the horses' heads lifting suddenly out of sleep, turning to check him.

With a forty-watt glow now defining the shadows, Ambelin moves to the stall of his favourite, an Anglo-Arab gelding named Bacchanal, out of Chintz by Romeo, showing great promise.

So he has a zealous look in his eye.

He talks in a slow voice to this fine, tall specimen of a horse as it wheels with a barely repressed energy around its stall . . . he is utterly convinced: of what he is saying, and that it understands.

Bacchanal eyes him with a watchful certainty.

'Perfection, aren't you, you great big thing, you?' he enquires.

The horse flicks its ears and turns away – as though it's heard this before.

Moon sidles warily round, keeping an eye on the bigger animal.

Ambelin admires the gloss on Baccanal's coat. 'Kind of a wild thing, huh?'

He puts his hand under the sweat rug and smooths its rump, sensing the power under the skin – the potential frenzy of running under there; it is so urgent to run, this horse sometimes gets so urgent. His own muscles are shrinking, loosening on the bone . . .

He withdraws his hand.

Muscle!

If he thinks just for a moment – what could he make of muscle? Incredible. Could it be believed, the design of a muscle? Mechanised instinct; Nature; the engine of existence – but he himself is running down, perhaps.

Just to have the time and inclination to think like this is – is a *relief* . . .

For instance, the meaning of life?

Bacchanal grinds his jaws loudly on the hay and swivels a suspicious look back to Ambelin Sayers.

He is soft for the horse because it's mute. It offers no answer; what's more it doesn't even ask the question, and if it doesn't ask, then maybe it knows . . .

The horse leaves off considering him, turning to its feed. Ambelin feels a little hurt.

(Against his will he is given a brief picture of Amie's face: the door closing across it – her look of alarm. He wills the door shut.)

Like a painter desirous of creating a perfect landscape, he has been able to fill in, uproot and move people, block some out, bring his two close by; for that at least he must thank the practicality of money.

Ambelin walks on the moss peat littering the floor. It has an unpredictable give in it, which makes progress difficult.

Moon follows, still nervous.

Hearing Bacchanal's swallow, Ambelin remembers he didn't finish his food. Too much excitement. Bad for him . . . he thinks about eating – eating's a swap, that's all it is: life for death. Good luck if you're the right side of the deal, bad luck for something, someone else on the other side. He didn't finish . . . He doesn't mind, any more, whether he eats or gets eaten.

Outside, above their heads, the sky thunders a complaint: the weight of this blundering, eyeless summer storm.

Ambelin thinks on, about the mystery, the question why Nature evolves towards death, why his life is spinning out its last few repeat patterns; why cruelty is so much the order of things, so even his success has been cruel to him; how he's well down the way to dying, but how everything, even the newest-born baby, is (equally) tipped towards death, but also towards renewal.

Moon's scared of the horse. She sits with her back pressed uncomfortably hard against the woodwork, still keeping Bacchanal's switching tail in sight. She is ready to escape whatever happens, but gives Ambelin a brief welcome now he's reached her side of the stall.

Over here it's unsoiled, the crumbling blanket of peat moss, a paler brown under his feet.

So he sits next to Moon and leans his back against the wooden slats. Some of them have gotten chewed, in places, by various animals over the years.

Resting his head, he finds the high rafters in his line of sight and checks along a row of frizzle bantams trying to sleep up there, perched right under the noise of the rain.

There had been a sick one once, called after its illness.

He calls, softly, 'Fowlpest.'

Two of them peel back bottom eyelids. But he wouldn't be able to recognise it now . . . too long ago.

He digs himself deeper into the peat moss.

A musty fragrance.

The horse pauses in its chewing, then comes a gulp as it swallows. The long jaws continue working.

With something like wonder, Ambelin feels a tiredness approaching.

After a while he closes his eyes.

The rain drums comfortingly.

AMIE MOSS and her son TJ aren't too much part of the West Virginia community. No one says it but they should have a bit more money, be somewhere smarter, a state where they forbid roadside hoardings, where everyone has an old family lakehouse to go for a summer break. It would suit their accents better. And they harbour privacy, which isn't done by townfolk here, where Southern openness is more than a crack ajar; only the hill people have that stare for strangers that TJ has when they walk by and he's popping baskets using his childhood plastic loop or repeatedly pitching to a white spot marked on the garage wall.

Amie, particularly, excites a sense of difference in her neighbours. For sure, no one else buys alcohol through mail order. No one lost their house since Jimmy Ether forgot to pay tax for four years.

This week of the final packing up, some people make it their business to offer help.

When she returned from her encounter with Ambelin Sayers after a stopover in NYC for two days (one day to drink at Harry's and the other to recover from drink) the first thing she saw was TJ, sitting on the two-brick-high rim which contains the square of lawn in front of their home, digging gravel from the treads of his shoes. When he stood up, pulling the Sayers height on her, she felt bounced, surrounded by this rare breed of man (only two left). Whichever way she turns she is running to or from a Sayers, whacked from the older, more troublesome one to this secret, younger one – any direction she takes means discomfort. But, she tells herself, one of them is her own and the other she'll never have to mix with again.

Now, two weeks later, during which time she's been out of favour with TJ for refusing to tell him where she went, she's still coping with difficulties: the packing-up of houseware she doesn't want to leave for the tenant's use; TJ's anti-reaction to both of her suggestions as to where they should go – he objects to Arthur Cinsaretti's offer of help and he protests at going to the decrepit lakehouse that's been in her family since her grandparents' time.

Meanwhile, as an additional undertow, continually worry-ing, Amie has to juggle the last few sums of money: the tenants' deposit equals her arrears on the mortgage of her mortgage; the enforced pay-off from the medical-equipment company could null her Mastercard and American Express bills at a stroke but it might have to be called on (if they take the lakehouse option) as a means to live for the next four months; her car, however, is not worth anything because rust has eaten away at the metal which supports the top of the suspension dampers.

This has capped her hatred for the vehicle.

The poorer she becomes the more she's intimate with each possession, its condition, its likely durability, the exact quality of satisfaction it can give to their lives or the measure of trouble it may cause.

TJ's not helping, what with this insisting on being called a name different from the one he was christened with.

Poised around a collection of cardboard boxes in the upstairs landing of their home, she asks, again, 'Please, TJ.'

'My name's *not* TJ.'

The boy is sulking. It suits him.

He's taken to wearing a downbeat overcoat so long it nearly sweeps the ground. As he moves it scoops air and billows like a sail. He is circling the boxes, his newly masculine head nodding heavily with each step, throwing glances sideways (never given for long). He looks unstable – she's sure he cultivates this impression, he's playing at being a poet or a nascent revolutionary or a philosopher, an outsider type (he's currently emerging from an interest in transvestite mur-derers). Despite herself, she is excited by the idea of so much potential in the man-to-come. A big stack of time in front of

56

him. A fast brain in there – she likes to think she's objective about his intelligence. Sometimes she catches herself hardly able to wait for the next thing he might say or do, his next piece of news, a true friend or a girl, surely, soon . . .

Amie Moss says, 'You've been TJ for the last fifteen years so that's what I'm calling you.'

'Major peeve, Mom, my name's *Hero*.' His mother's hands are shaking and she's wearing make-up. Together these two factors can only add up to one thing: the man he's not yet seen, the man called Arthur, is due here, or Arthur's going to get a visit from his mother, the probable location for the meeting is the Carvery – in his hotel. She met Arthur at the store, they must have been behaving like people in 'Frisco, like in that movie. To TJ, it smells stupid.

'Please, it's got to be done and I can't do it.'

She repeats, 'I can't do it, TJ.'

'I know *that*,' he replies.

She's got the ladders ready and pointing up at the dark square of the opened trap, but TJ refuses to co-operate.

'I don't want to go with Arthur and his car. And I don't want to go to the . . . the . . .' (he decides not to swear in front of his mother) 'the beep lakehouse.'

'You always liked it.'

'Not to *live* in. I like Sugar Oats and cold milk, doesn't mean I want to go live in the *box* with them.'

'Well, we might not have to go.' She's favouring the Arthur Cinsaretti option, now.

She adds, 'Some of the time, you know, some of the time it's best just to get on and do what your mom says, TJ.'

'It's building to major gloominess, Mom, calling me the wrong name. I'm *Hero*.'

She winces under the resentful stare from the boy. His disapproval makes her hop with mixed-up feelings, always. She craves instant forgiveness from him and a return to an affectionate state, but she knows she has a responsibility not to be weak and she's stretched already, in other ways, for the sake of heaven she's wretched enough without bowing, being ashamed of herself.

His terrible power over her.

She watches his pacing.

'Hero, life cannot continue until you put those fucking boxes up there in the roof,' she claims, simply. She'll stand her ground here. She feels weary.

To pass the time she looks at her nails, freshly painted. At her age she needs all the help she can get.

She allows herself a daydream: it's all working out with Arthur Cinsaretti, him driving up in his clean car, TJ greeting him enthusiastically. Then after a bit the two of them, old man and young, doing things together, in an unconsidered way.

TJ's still not answering.

She extends the vision of hopefulness: herself at peace, with a view of hills – uncultivated meadowland. Sunlight creeping on her bare legs. The absolving of grief and guilt. Ambition just – well, on the way to being granted. Needs answered. Cleanliness. Health. A lighter hunger – and the means to answer it in precisely the right way. Affection granted in small episodes, doses of the stuff which are capable of moving her surprisingly powerfully.

Why *not*? Why shouldn't this have happened, or be about to happen?

But it's a familiar process, refusing herself any pity. She is not allowed it, she has to coach her attitude: she must think

58

she wanted to drink this house away, she intended, decided to, because if she indulges in blaming other things, even for a moment, things like cruel fate or lost love (her favourites), it will bring a resumption of drinking.

When she's going dry the whole of life comes at her through the bottom of a glass.

She watches as TJ takes his coat off and carefully folds it over the back of a chair.

'I'll do it for fifteen . . . thousand . . . bucks,' suggests TJ, stroking a bit of fluff from the coat.

Amie turns under the anger. 'Oh I get it. Point taken.' This brings back the shakes which had partially subsided during her daydream and she's working it out already – because his every suggestion has to be questioned, even his humour has to be deconstructed. But she's fed up with such *analysis*. Just to eat, sleep, see him, to get the odd touch of familiarity from him. Respect is too much to ask for, she reminds herself, a violent realisation that could do for her if she didn't judge that sometimes she does have his respect (curiously enough, not when she's going dry – she could spend time wondering about that).

The only rule he's made for her: no lying. This makes her unlike any other alcoholic and she's grateful (to end up owing someone so young is a matter of shame).

TJ says, 'Plus an extra ten thousand bucks for closing the trap and cleaning up the floor here.'

She still gets surprised sometimes that someone as straight-forward, nice, capable and funny as herself should want to drink. It's someone else in her, a parasite soul, saddened, doing this drinking. She talks with it, always the same topic: giving up. She tries cajoling. When she's on a binge she gets

59

religious about it: drink is her devil and she imagines her devil's hand – hairy, knurled, with such strength – forcing her, emptying her purse, turning her decisions, altering her erratic path. The evidence in the garage. Once, drunken, she had actually laughed, watching the heap of bottles grow to ridiculous proportions. It was a hopeless moment: as tenants were going to occupy the house she thought TJ and she might end up living in there. It would be a Herculean task: The Clearing-Out of Amie's Garage.

'Well . . .' suggests Amie, 'give me a discount, huh? Fifteen thousand all in? Including cleaning up? That would be manageable.'

Amie is thick-skinned. The one advantage to having a major fucking-up of your life is that it drowns minor embarrassments.

'Call it twenty thousand bucks including discount, Ma. The big two-oh, oh-oh-oh.'

'That includes the garage, Hero,' she replies, vengefully.

Silence.

'Mom, the garage? You are joking. You can*not* afford me. You cannot *beep* afford me.'

WIK SLAVERY, wearying of the papers in front of him, leans back in his chair.

He pictures himself as though he's someone else, looking down from a long way off: a man slumped in a new office in the Lakeside wing of the Blue House (all of which is currently being remodelled), exhausted from what can only be called homework.

Although these are days of triumph for him, he's not sure he's made the right choice – but it would take a fifty-metre run just to escape from this side of the house.

His fingers cruise over the desk as he tries to keep up with the speed of this thing.

Operational control of one half of the Corporation's interests around the world is being transferred to him, day by day, in a series of briefings given by executives, technicians and scientists, subject-expert in various of the Sayers ventures, all flown in from different locations around the world. This operation is labelled 'Utmost Secret' because the news (he can see it: WIK SLAVERY IS NEW SAYERS CEO BY HALF-MEASURE), when it strikes, must cause minimum loss of credibility.

Perhaps he shouldn't have chosen to be Keyman after all. It's as though he's a king without clothes: top-flight controllers, men and women whose mettle has been proven in the big, long, fight between plus and minus which has been the practical, moral and esoteric quiddity of any play of business since trade began, are coming and handing to him a respect he doesn't deserve because he has been put up by Ambelin Sayers. If they have reservations it doesn't show.

He could have chosen, as Buddy Maze did, non-executive directorships – to take the money and run.

But Wik can't take being given anything.

Sitting, this Sunday morning, in an oasis of quiet, he hears that something, again – like a faraway laugh . . .

For the second time he listens intently, relaxing only after a long enough spate of silence.

The office surrounds him, a comfort because he ordered the fitting himself, this part of the house being remodelled in his image. A Japanese influence is evident; the thinness of the style suits his own light elegance. He can have no complaints – it's exactly as he ordered it. The matching Staidadt chairs are in a crimson so dark that the red wavelength shows only in a rare wink of detail. The uppity technology is hidden in an elaborately engineered system of cabinets in the panelling.

He ticks it off, all this: good, excellent . . .

There – he hears it again, the distant noise, a niggling thing that threatens to upset him: is it someone. . . ?

It's particularly maddening, the sound, because it's only just audible, a small but insane – yes – *laugh*.

Coming from . . .?

He's up and on the trot, out of the office, turning right, following the noise. Meanwhile he counts the hours left that he can call his own because in the evening two men (one younger, with a sheaf of patent applications at the ready, the other older and scientific) will arrive to coach him on Sayers' investment of time and money in the development of water as a propellent fuel for motor vehicles . . . the separation of hydrogen and oxygen will be the small talk . . .

Unaccountably (because it was seven months ago), as he strides along, his metal heels cracking against the marble inlay of the central Lakeside corridor (more of a deserted avenue than a thoroughfare), he remembers his birthday and the fact that he only got three cards and one of them was sent by the Eagle Insurance Co. Inside their tastefully scripted congratulation on his birthday was a reminder that when (next year) he reaches the age of thirty-five, he will no longer be able to enjoy 'special premium return' on any life insurance he might take out. So they're telling him he's dying already.

The second card was from his therapist and the third was

from his estranged wife, the two children and their dogs all packed in together.

He reaches the Italian indoor garden which has an eight-foot-high engraved trellis (netted) forming a stylish membrane between house and aviary.

As he suspected, it is a bird. A parrot . . . of some sort, he thinks, peering into the sunlit interior, where the indoor trees (some sadly capped by a glass and timber roof) make a playground for a hundred exotic species.

He hears it clearly, yes, similar to a laugh, except that when the cry falls off to a silence it sounds like the tail end of an emergency siren (one weary of disaster).

Wik repeats to himself: it is only imitative, he will be able to ignore . . .

Could this destroy the viability of his new office? Hell, he will need to concentrate.

Maybe something can be done.

He turns on his heel, breaking off abruptly in the middle of a string of curses. Of course. It's simple. He asks . . .

Heading for Driveside (to find Ambelin) he reconsiders the curious thing that happened the previous day. (He's outside now, beaten by Sunday sun, flanking the yew hedge that addresses the rear of the house.) He was in the car, accompanying a certain Rodrigo Cuellar (dealer in drawings, ace at finding, somehow, studies of Old Masters among the leaves of derelict long-dead students' work-books), but he was not listening, though he should have been because this was a continuation of his briefing, which had run over into the time allotted for the drive to the Sayers jet, half an hour away; instead he purposefully manoeuvred himself to a position behind the chauffeur's right shoulder where he could frame himself in the rear-view mirror, so he was tucking his chin down and flirting with himself, playing sophisticated with this international art-speak going on, when the lowering sun flashed insolently in the glass. After this yellow panel of lightning momentarily crossed him he checked himself more closely; he noticed that one eye looked different from the other. In the left-hand one the same frightened infant was evident (as was always) but in the other – what he saw caused him a jump in charm and power, enough to demote the art-speak into something as insignificant as a distant unheeded radio voice, because he couldn't recognise the character behind it – it was as though someone else had been magically glazed on by the heat, perhaps, except the unrecognisable soul was more than superficially grafted, it was riding behind the pupil and dangerously in control.

It – that yesterday – had thrown him into a real half-and-half paranoia.

Now, on his way to Ambelin's haunt, Wik is passing the Driveside pond – he always checks the plainly smooth surface for any insect that might be tickling, causing ripples.

He only has to mention the parrot to Ambelin Sayers and something will get done?

The aviary can be moved, perhaps.

He strides into the Driveside wing, down corridors still unfamiliar. Doorways flash by. Men are working in every room. Under his orders.

So onwards, newly confident of his righteousness, and out the other side of the house. Right through the Coach-House gates. Into the yard.

The old man's face, turning under the sunlight, breaks up with smiles, every wrinkle lifting. Ambelin Sayers.

The famous recluse, ex-Chairman of the Sayers Corporation, is cooing affectionately.

'Wik, Wik . . . you know Moon of course . . .' He waves at the dog, who is drenched, glittering, standing in a tub of tepid water.

'Yes . . .'

'You know,' says Ambelin, holding out his painfully thin elbows, 'I am becoming more and more like the man in the oatmeal ads.'

Behind him Moon escapes from her bath and shakes herself, her legs skedaddling. The spray makes a temporary fountain, brilliant but short-lived.

Ambelin has wetness patched on his clothes. 'Not quite as homely a figure, mind you, as him.' From his height he peers down, all white skin stretched over bones, then slackened off a point or two, trying to good-humour Wik. 'More insanitary, that's for sure. You seen those pristine check shirts he wears? You know what? I haven't changed my clothes in two days. Just get up and put the same ones back on as before and come right out here, smelling less and less like oatmeal, I dare say.'

Moon wanders up. She doesn't stop, but gently charges Wik Slavery's groin. She's always been interested in the front of people's trousers.

Wik disguises a swift batting-sideways of the dog as an energetic stroke of its jaws.

'Woop, Moon likes you,' observes Ambelin.

Wik Slavery yawns.

'Say, you OK? You must be whacked, all that stuff you're taking on.'

Wik denies anything, 'No, no . . .'

'You know what, I clap my own back over this, over what I've done. Never have thought good of myself before.'

He adds, 'It's not the cleverest thing I ever did, but hell, the stupidest thing not to have done it before.'

Ambelin Sayers' smile is still in the practice stage.

Wik Slavery feels his resolve thin down by half. Politeness checks his purpose.

'Ambelin . . .' he begins. 'I was hoping . . .'

Moon again offers her nose up to the front of his trousers. She's going to find something of real interest . . .

Ambelin says, 'Moon likes you! She knows all right . . .'

'Ah . . .'

'I'm sorry. You were hoping . . .?'

Wik Slavery has to chuck Moon under the chin hard enough to lift her out of there. The dog's two front paws are now off the ground because she's levering her nose down.

Ambelin's concerned at his dog's rudeness. 'Moon, over here, c'mon out of it.'

He adds, 'I'm sorry.'

'She's a beautiful dog.'

Moon backs off.

'Isn't she? Now, you still OK to come do a round with me Thursday?'

'Sure.'

'It would be good, too, if we drove back via the east side of the lake and took a look in at the marina, check if *Hero* is OK?'

'Sure, why not.'

'I haven't looked her over in ages. We could take her out next week?'

'I'd like that,' replies Wik Slavery.

Moon goes in again *underneath* his hand. Wik gives a brace

of heavy pats to the top of her head, pressing down hard. Moon persists, squirming in (so much resistance means there's something there).

Wik feels Moon's eyelash flutter against his thumb. He cranks his thumb inwards and skates his nail into the jelly of the dog's eye.

Moon is beaten by this cruelty. One eye is clamped, leaking water; the other is blinking furiously. She lifts a wet paw, waves it, staggers, lowers it to save balance. She can't see a thing. She rubs it against the underside of her leg.

Ambelin doesn't notice.

His height causes him embarrassment, sometimes he wishes he were closer to the ground, with elbows and knees more in line and co-ordinated. 'Wik,' he begins, 'I wonder, you mind if I mention something?'

Wik is asking himself why everything can't be straightforward. Why can't he say what he wants? Instead of, 'No, go ahead.'

'I was reading this, and I thought it's important, that if – between friends, you understand – if it goes wrong, if there's something up, then people should be used to speaking, talking to one another, about it. What d'you think?' Ambelin waits with unashamed admiration for the enlightenment and concurrence that he's convinced is about to come over his friend.

Wik Slavery nods thoughtfully and draws a breath, but says nothing.

Ambelin says, 'I'm no expert psychologist, but it feels right.'

'Sure, I agree, absolutely,' Wik manages eventually.

Ambelin makes a gesture like he's batting away an insect. 'Luckily there's nothing wrong!'

'No . . .'

Ambelin Sayers feels cheered.

IN NEW ORLEANS it's so hot the music hardly sweats out onto the pavements in the daytime, because this year there's not enough money, it's not loose enough in people's pockets to bribe the musicians to tire themselves out in the heat. At night the French quarter throngs with expectation – much of it answered with trash-rock numbers and fake jazz for the tourists, who can't understand why the police behave so brutally, but if you know where to go there's excitement, and that's why the police are so cruel: hired in to walk the same side of the line as Voodoo, drug-dealing and corruption, they lash out, part of that scene.

Buddy Maze is too well known a figure here, which is why this Tuesday afternoon finds him heading towards Megaton, the most expensive clothes store in the city – expensive not just because it fits outsize men, but also it's decided to be expensive, nestling as it does between other rich shops in the newish luxury mall down on the river, converted from warehousing. Buddy's getting out of New Orleans, but in style.

The whole complex is deserted, he's almost a lone customer. His opulent figure is spied on hopefully by the fragrance salespeople and others on commission while the salaried ladies and gentlemen manning the smart stores are purposefully too busy refolding linen shirts or doodling seasonal concepts for their own (very *individual*) windows.

In Megaton they receive him like a king, hastening to service such a large and busy purchaser.

In the quadruple-size changing booth Buddy plants his mobile and hooks up the fistful of laden hangers. He begins to strip off from the shoes upwards. Used clothing he flings under the bench.

He thinks, La Paz (Ambelin's Mexican ocean home).

He remembers someone – one of a crew of new people surrounding him – advising, 'Get plenty of light stuff, if you're buying for La Paz.'

His trousers land in the heap.

What can he do for Ambelin? It's going to be important to keep the man sweet because this tax-evasive gifting pro-gramme is a bit-by-bit, year-by-year transfer of Ambelin's wealth and Buddy's thinking is that while one year's hit is worth a fortune by anyone's standards, he wants as many fortunes as he can get before the old man goes. Hell, if he only has one fortune, it might get taken away from him.

So whatever they do together, he and Ambelin, it's got to be healthy. Maybe they can eat together at places where the table napkins come made of white linen as stiff as cardboard, where people talk about important stuff, where all the waitresses are high-born and filling in until they meet someone; he and Ambelin can buy real safe luxury cars and ride around; they can buy a boat and cruise off La Paz with experienced deckhands working the route while they're on the fishing rods, but securely strapped in with all the fancy tackle, belts and other bits of gear and suchlike (women serving them); they can go together and pass muster round some Hollywood pool-parties . . . He sees in his mind's eye a swollen pair of breasts on a woman good enough to put up with anything.

Naked, he pulls on a cotton square underwear piece ('for

the whole man'). Because of the steeply reversed gradient from his navel down to his groin the elastic fails to grip at the front, merrily sliding downhill, stopped only by the projection, at the back, of his deceptively innocent and affecting buttocks.

He will order two dozen in different colours.

This shopping gig is because he wants to take nothing with him, not a stitch nor a speck of dust on the bottom of a shoe, from his old life. When he reaches La Paz, bound for secrecy's sake to reside there until press day at least (which should be easy, it's nothing short of a sand palace after all), he wants to be new, to start again as the character he was meant to have been a long time before now.

All the suits he's chosen are of linen. He has a taste for the crumpled, busy look.

His anxiousness to begin loosening up on the new money is an itch in the palms of his hands. He shakes out some trousers. He'll buy them anyway. Just for the belt. Just for the hell of it.

He thinks of the deal he's made: he got them together, his side of Sayers, and told them he was lazy. They were to give him a non-executive whatsit, same salary, plus inflation, plus ten, plus stay-payment bonuses, the houses, the boat.

A new life . . . and he will be a freshly cut figure. Reinsured from top to toe: autos all comprehensive, life cover, health, old age, personal accident, the lot. Expensively settled in the sand palace, fast and mobile with cars and boats and planes. Rewardrobed here, and elsewhere for the shoes. A legal team to be the fist for any bullying he might want to do. There's some top women out there, also, who'll have noses for men like him.

He resents it that he'll have to use his old passport, even. He wants a different, more valuable name.

He especially resents that when he's finished here, got into the back seat of the limo, turned up the cold air, maybe taken in a little TV or watched the public trying to stare in through the one-way glass, or bought himself some ass, OK up to there, but then he'll have to go home and tell his one-breasted *wife* that he still very definitely *loves* her?

The thought of her having a handle on half of him (because of a pre-nuptial that he himself had engineered, of all the ironies) is hateful.

'Boo-fuckin'-hoo,' he mumbles, his bottom lip jutting out so it matches the corpulence, for a moment, of his earlobes.

Just to compensate, he might have to go and buy a . . . something, anything . . .

IN THE HUNTING life of the financial media there's occasionally a hiatus, when they have no secret. The large public relax and enjoy a brief few days of wholly predictable mid-term results and new appointments. However, the professional chasers know that somewhere there's a happening they should know about.

Experienced Sayers-watchers have marked the delay in handing over to the long-nominated Keyman. They saw half of Ambelin Sayers' titling, CEO, dribble down to Jack Cavendish at the AGM over a year ago, the classic sign of his preferment – but now Jack's sitting by a swimming pool, piqued, with an unusable directorship. The prorogation is a warning; those for whom no press release is worded carefully enough, who listen to silences, who can read their own intuition and who have the measure of Ambelin Sayers know that the stay on the hand-over is an ethereal barrier surrounding a secret. Journalists and commentators are watching out for where it's going to open up, when the big event is going to break surface, whom it's best to be with and where. They follow standard intelligence-gathering techniques, calling the ring of people – first the dealer, then the mole, then the analyst, then, pretending to be either an academic working on a study or a shareholder, they try the company itself. So, although everyone can see Sayers is in play, it reads confused, going red and blue by turns – that most valuable of financial commodities, *true* information, is not breaching the Chinese walls between dealers, bankers and analysts.

The secret is known by twenty-nine people. Take this one time and it could be found in the breast pocket of a Seal suit, in a briefcase lying on a Regency chair, in a guarded call from a toll phone to avoid the dealers' tapes, between the lines of a letter written on Sayers paper, in the gaps between various conversations; it has a reverse presence in the briefings that don't happen and it will make an appearance, later on, lurking underneath the mysterious postponement of certain projects. All those who have the secret know its financial import and what it will do for them personally; warily (because the law reins in on the opportunities here) they plan PA business, spreading risks small and wide among the less important brokers, dealing always below the ten-thousand-dollar threshold where the legal radar doesn't go, knowing which dealers to run with, and how far.

Meanwhile, outside of the twenty-nine who know and the professional players who know they don't know, the masses rise to the same sun, driving or walking to work, carried by necessity mostly, chewing up sneakers on the broken sidewalks of big cities, wearing down the stairs of their homes and offices, trotting through subways, running out of freeways, consuming, breeding, grasping at rainbow-coloured happiness, feeling it sometimes in themselves as a vibration but more often, more strongly, glimpsing it in a girl's smile flashed from the side window of a fast-accelerating, nearly-new car – and most of them, for the moment oblivious, ignorant only because of the deliberate, legal secrecy in the chains of corporate nomenclature, have a share in this without knowing it.

The secret shows its face shyly for such a monster, only when the lights are as out as they ever are in cities and business is complete on the east coast; people asleep; it's outed by a 'source' and suddenly it's on the DJ wire, unattributed – from whence the secret springs, even, is secret. Immediately it pulls wild interest. So many fingers poking at phone buttons is like the concentrated digging of a terrier at its prey's earthen hole. The hunt is on. Behind the hunt comes the machinery of support (paying the bill). Sayers stock in Japan begins to go deep red. London dealers read their Topic screens and prepare to empty their boots.

So TV screens buzz into life. Everyone channel-hops. The media are beating down on it: numerous voices, spoken and written.

On Channel 2 a young talking-head parrots in a near-hysterical delivery; she looks into the line of the camera but she's still supremely aware that it's not a single lens but hundreds of millions of people watching her. She reports that as soon as the market opened in Tokyo, Sayers dropped like a stone, getting wiped as she speaks.

There have been crowd scenes all night: lights for the video news wash the reflective faces with white, making it look cold out there, panicky as well because the wind lifts people's hair. One strange face is shouting again and again every half-hour on Channel 2, 'Nothing. Nothing. What do I do? Someone tell me what to do. Someone tell me where my money *is*?' He tilts his head from side to side. 'I had it, now it's gone. De da, de da. They write and tell you you got this much, now they tell you, you'll have nothing. So who's got it?' The man slaps the back of one hand into the palm of the other. 'Who's got it right now? Is it my fault? No. Is it someone else's fault? Yes. Who's got my money *right now*?'

Some more rational conversations are taking place, voices tried by experience, measured, fitted with calm analysis; on one show they're inverting the stock phrasing on its head and asking, 'What goes down, must come back up again? Can that be something we can look forward to in the short to medium term?'

Then the reply: 'I don't think so. If the team isn't in place, then it won't happen. If a team *were* to be installed, you'd be talking crisis management . . .'

Renewed attention is paid to Ambelin Sayers and what it is, exactly, that's made him successful. The fall is so fast and hard because of people's inflated belief in him, he's not perceived as a businessman but as a magician, a sodium crumb buzzing with so many maverick interests, consuming, leading him here and there, the lawyers sweeping up deals behind him, accruing legend. He had the ability to make money without trying and he kept on making more of it, thus inspiring a spiritual level of confidence. He led the market, unknowing, a genie; suddenly he's taken himself out of it.

But of all the people seized on, Wik Slavery is hounded the

74

most because he's new. And the size of the story: someone who just gave the old man a ride? Now he's CEO of half of Sayers? The Singhalese analyst, excited financial darling of Channel 5, claims, 'We have to recognise the baldness of this. Sayers is split down the middle, one half controlled by a respectable management team, the other with this new CEO Keyman, Wik Slavery. But Slavery is . . .' The man waves his hands. 'He's a nobody. That's a bad mistake. He has to go. It is up to the Executive. The Executive needs to think straight on this one and ask themselves whether or not the situation can be repaired . . .'

They find Wik Slavery that same night in a club on 57th, spending money freely to keep people near him, not having to talk because of the volume of the music, his looks and new money working for him. With more and more people eyeing him from the door (some getting cameras taken off them?) and coming straight over, he registers that a change has occurred, a sudden largeness in the ambience opens up and he is being looked at like he's the one expected to fall into it.

When a certain level of confusion is reached, with strangers' mouths opening in front of him and the closest girl looking frightened by the crush, he finds himself on the way out, borne by a loose but concerted opinion, held it seems by everyone, that he has to go. When he hits the door fireworks go off in a spectacular array and he can see only silhouettes moving, lifting cameras to eyelines, as the flashing blinds him and now someone's got his hand and he's lost control of where he can go.

The pictures hit every front cover during the following week, printed with varying degrees of quality and trimmed differently, but all using the same image: most of the space is taken with the figure of the girl caught with her tongue resting on her teeth and her show-off skirt rucked up around a thigh dimpled with fat, a loopy breast escaping, and a hand stretched back to hold him up. His own face only comes into the picture from the side, like some drunk. His mouth is open and his eyes stare because, although it can't be understood from the photograph, he is actually falling to the ground.

THERE ARE SOME who think they're immune to the Sayers débâcle. Amie Moss can even hope (idly, only, because of a history of disappointment in miracles) that the downward-spinning numbers she hears about on TV (without understanding exactly what they are or *do*) might catch at her debt figure and pull it along; her petty disaster would, perhaps, be swamped by the larger one, dissolve and disappear. She'll keep quiet.

Arthur Cinsaretti is wrathful, holding onto an unfounded righteousness; were he to be in charge of these affairs everything would run smoothly, but anyway he's paid off his houses and cars (he has a fundamentalist's belief in not having debts or credits) and since he has only just reshuffled his futures (he calls them 'mah date with fate'), their sell-bys are far enough ahead in time to allow him hope that all this will pan out and things stay on a rise for him. Nevertheless, about to undertake the journey home to Oregon with Amie and her son TJ, both of them alive, kicking, open-mouthed with poverty and his responsibility now, he catches himself thinking that he will increase the size of his vegetable garden (always a sign of bad nerves).

76

And there are more fleshly worries, as they discuss their plans for the near future.

Arthur is stabled (as he calls it) in the Resting House Hotel, the route to which Amie has become depressingly familiar with – five times now she has visited him driving this, her one remaining car (what remains of it), turning left, right, left round the back of the rent-all place, finding the lowered lip on the sidewalk to ease her retread tyres up onto the forecourt, parking in the same slot, dreading the knowledgeable smile of the receptionist whom she is expecting to greet her by name if she walks past just one more time.

Arthur Cinsaretti suits his hotel room. They have things in common: a preoccupation with appearance, a bland understanding of basic needs. Both have a similar effect on others: a tickling suspicion that, although everything looks expensive, something is going to be annoying, not work properly.

Amie Moss, standing behind him, has the brief privacy needed to inspect again the paint on her fingernails. Red. She can't get used to them. As though touched with blood. They look capable of anything, now.

Although she dislikes make-up.

Mr Cinsaretti is snapping his jacket lapels; he knows it won't change the shape of his body – that wouldn't be possible however many hands were put to work on the cut of the cloth – but it's a habit and he likes keeping his habits. He turns to her, smiling, sucks in his belly and straightens the trim of his trouser-band.

'A regular moment of prayer,' he announces, 'is what's needed to keep things straight between people.'

She feels pinned down, although he is clear across the other side of the room with reproduction furniture positioned like staging posts between them.

'Not that I am not prey to the temptations of the flesh,' admits Mr Cinsaretti. 'Having been a victim in the past of the looks of a woman, of the allure of her shape, of the touch of a female hand – I know these sensations.' Arthur's aware he's not got sleek looks or a charming way, but one of the reasons he believes in God is that there's a hand pushing him into doing things, whether he likes it or not.

Amie will need to defend herself physically at some stage, she is sure of that. Isn't she worse than TJ? He would simply finger the man's wallet and take the Vantage card and the cash. She's after the same thing, isn't she, but first she has to touch the man's heart? So, the make-up mirror gets the old talc dusted off it and lipstick covers her rueful smile. (It's only her complexion, the rest is in good shape and works well on men.) She prefers a range of products packed under the trade-name 'Mask'. The name is fitting, although she suspects it's exactly the same as the stuff she once used called 'Joy'. These names and the make-up and her predicament – she's aware of playing because she can do nothing but string him along, she will finally refuse him.

Arthur Cinsaretti has reached the trouser press.

'For instance,' he says, 'the Bible forbids sexual intercourse before marriage. Now, I can do that, I can, but not without difficulty, not without prayer.'

He adds, 'And not without additional help from the woman.'

She thinks, Negotiation. 'Arthur, can we talk about this some other time? All I got on my mind is you meeting up with TJ. I can't talk about anything else 'til that's all done, you know, out of the way? Everybody happy?'

78

Arthur considers her request, then says, 'Let me tell you a story.'

He is unnecessarily smoothing the bald part of his scalp, which erupts from the fringe of fine hair encircling it.

'I had a friend, a real good friend, and he was engaged to be married to a fine woman.' He nods his head, judging her again. 'A fine woman.'

He stops at the mock-cane rocking chair. He hasn't had sex for a long time.

'So they have a date set for the wedding. And of course they don't want to . . . don't want to consume each other, before that day. They are aware that the eyes of the Lord are looking down and the eyes of the Lord, unlike our own, can see everywhere, in every intimate place, mental or physical.'

Amie flinches. The Lord might be prising open her knees.

'But,' continues Arthur Cinsaretti, 'they . . .' He stops to consider the most respectful way of saying this. 'They *managed*. D'you see? They managed.' He smiles benignly.

She considers him. 'Arthur, I must say, I must tell you, if I appear cold, it's not because . . . well, I got a son, you know, I'm not all the way a novice at that sort of thing.' She does return his smile, then. She likes the impossible confidence of this man sometimes. 'I understand, Arthur.'

It's as though he hasn't heard her – he's got to finish the fable. 'Course he kinda got a taste for oral intercourse after that.' He delivers this as though it were a mere postscript to the relating of a friend's engagement. 'Weird, but true, he kinda got a taste for it.'

'I do see, yes.'

He's close enough now for her to spot the shine on his lip, slicked there by a wet tongue, wiped across fast. Arthur's

79

frightened of making a mistake but he has to carry on.

'You're a fine woman,' he warns.

She's stuck, with this arm coming out towards her. She allows it to slide around her shoulder. With a bump his stomach arrives. She must allow him this.

Now both hands are sliding down her back. A squeeze. She resists an impulse towards anger.

Suddenly oral sex with Arthur seems funny. His cheek is tickling her and his hands are moving like a schoolboy's.

'Arthur,' she whispers, 'I've got some toothache. I don't think I can right now.'

EVERYTHING'S MADE sore by a day of sunshine – now the dusk is broken up with slivers of strange colour. Ambelin Sayers is preparing the evening feed. The trolley is built by Yellowhammer, the avicultural specialists, with neat compartments for gravel, bonemeal, crushed shell, grain, bark, saltchips, nuts, crawling livefeed.

Moon scoots up through the skylight to lie in the gully (just wide enough for her body) between the two canted sides of the roof. This is her favourite position – from here she can overlook the yard. She lies with her front paws curled round the edge of the leadwork, her muzzle resting. She sees Ambelin, vaguely, or bits of him: an arm scooping and pouring, a leg standing with difficulty, cut off from its fellow by the vertical of the stockroom door.

She is exhausted from thinking about him.

Rolling onto her side, she stretches her jaw along the mild

80

warmth of the lead. A groan escapes – she is sated, too full with it: the chasing games, the questions, the striving.

Ambelin is unaffected by the furore surrounding the succession of Keyman Wik Slavery. Since the virtual kidnap of Wik that night, followed by a siege at his therapist's apartment on Gramercy Park, Wik has hidden himself away in the Lakeside wing of the house. Ambelin doesn't fret over this, he considers that the young man has had a shock from which he will recover given a spell of solitude, a place away from the press of events. Ambelin remembers the elastic optimism of his own youth . . . that's how it will be: Wik bouncing out of the mood, in due course. He has this benevolent, parental attitude to Wik's trauma because, after all, it's what he himself has been through many times. At first it frankly amused him to watch Wik's woundedness, but then he comforted him, telling the younger man that it wasn't much different from other rows he'd seen happen over the years. People get spooked too easily. And even if Wik were stood in the tatters of his last suit Ambelin considers that he would chase victory, wouldn't he? He's young, fit, full of ideas?

Besides, Ambelin counselled, failure has got a bad reputation, undeserved, because losing can be executed successfully. There is a certain grace to it, if done well, that immediately cancels its worst effects. People ought to fail more often, it opens doors, causes gaps to appear. These massagers of markets, running with opinion, they should see better than an old man like himself that if you speed up the market with computers then you electrify the panic, the holes get deeper, the highs higher, the turnarounds turn round quick as lightning. The confidence of the market has always been fragile on purpose: the market makes money out of its own instability, that's the market's job, how it pays its way, but the nuts and bolts still get banged out, the aircraft go on flying, the hotels are taking bookings, the newspapers are selling.

All this has been useful advice, from himself to Wik Slavery.

A frizzle cock crows in the late afternoon, so is something wrong?

Ambelin used to envy the man whose job this was, Headkeeper Johnson. Strange, how old Johnson ended up hating birds, thinking they were all stupid.

His knee is playing up – it's hard to lift himself aboard the toy-like tractor.

He pulls the throttle lever and enjoys it that the tick of the engine jumps to a high line of sound, steadying at maximum revolutions, which still only translates into a sedate speed round the Driveside of the Blue House. Bobbing on the miniature machine, the welds in his spine aching stiffly, he considers this: that he always wanted to learn to fly, had a feeling he could if he tried. This last day or two is the closest he's come to that sensation he used to enjoy: a belief that if he jumps from a high building he will not fall, but instead win an escape from gravity, a float in any direction, to any height.

He'd be a long, old bird, in a sky of his own.

His hermitage here at home with Moon and the other animals has brought him to a pitch of excitement: he watches the deepening division of colour on his arm (the bottom half browned by the sun) and thinks of himself as having been dipped to the elbows in soil.

Although he is still plagued by worry (it irritates the outside of him, he has to avoid it by sinking deeper in thought) over what he's *not* doing, he is still determined to value silence because it hasn't disappointed him.

Moon is trotting behind.

In his head Ambelin rehearses the co-ordination necessary for his favourite move: steering at maximum speed (the grip of his left thumb is a problem) through the double doors into the aviary, round the back of the triple-domed interior cages, ready for work. Some foodstuffs he will scatter haphazardly on the ground; some he will dribble into the traps; some he will have to climb ladders for, to reach the hanging points. Best of all is the handling of livefeed. He wonders what they think is happening, these grubs, as they crawl over and around one another to find no earth, nothing but more of themselves. He will drop them, a squirming mess, into the holes set in the ground, replacing the turf-covered lids to stop the bullying greenbacks from jumping in and gorging themselves as soon as he turns his back. Then he will feel like Father Christmas, wandering about releasing insects, morsels that will decorate the undergrowth, and enjoying the birds' chatter and their sharp looks. He approves of their distrust of him.

Rounding the side of the aviary (it looks like a space station tacked onto the side of this pile of a house), Ambelin Sayers sees a rectangular flag of glass and steel sticking out; the outside door is open. He thumps the steering wheel and curses himself. To make a mistake like that! He wonders if this happened because he's old.

Steering the tractor (four turns of the wheel), he sees that the inside door, too, is open. A flutter beats in his chest (a double beat, like wings).

Inside the first cage he kills the tractor engine and scrambles off the seat. His shin burns from where he cracked it against the clutch lever.

He stops still, looks, listens. Empty space. The perches are silent. Nothing moves.

Above him the foliage rests.

With a cry he notices that other doors are open – all three cages are empty. He stumbles through.

Nothing.

Maybe he's blind . . .

All gone?

Surely some would have remained . . . he plunges through the rattan thicket.

But to leave the doors open is not only to allow the birds to escape, it's also to let other animals in. A cat?

Moon follows Ambelin back and forth, listening to the silence, watching him as he sits on the tractor's wheelguard. She pads across and waits, but no attention to her is forthcoming. When he starts calling it's not directed at her. It's an angry noise. She is far from whatever's going on.

Who else has come in here? No one.

There's been no breach in security.

Dumbfounded, he replays the details of his morning visit. Was there any loss of memory or black spot in the line of time? He tries to remember leaving. How could *all* the doors be open? Is he making it up? He's not reliable any more – was that time he locked up yesterday or today?

It can't be anyone else's fault but his. Keeper Johnson – an old man, older than himself – did the job faultlessly for eleven and a half years.

They've escaped.

He trots outside and scours the darkening panorama.

Nothing.

He walks back inside. He feels dread and sickness. It occurs to him to telephone every neighbour, to hire an army of people.

It would be hopeless, he knows that.

He must confess to Wik.

He is up and slamming the glass doors. Repeatedly, on his way out. Between his hands he grips his old, useless, forgetful, broken-down head. Which quarter of it holds memory?

Once on the lawn he buckles up in anger, his ligaments cracking, still panning his sight back and forth, hoping for a glimpse of a dark spot fluttering through the gloom.

He blames old age. Some part of his brain slipped. Then, can he not trust himself to think about two things at once any more? He gets up off the warm grass.

His shouting can be heard from way off. And there's the throwing of kicks against the aluminium framework. He is a stick-like, ineffectual figure striking the side of a mansion worth more than the amount most people could earn if they were given five lifetimes.

'Sir, Mr Sayers . . .'

The old man is pushing the heels of his hands against the glass.

'I, I . . .' He is wound into the anger now.

The groundsman tries to intervene and Moon nips this other man's heel, unsure if it's real or a game – how hard to bite?

'They've been sold!'

Ambelin stops cold. 'What?'

'Mr Slavery's got a swimming pool lined up for in here.'

Ambelin gives him (the minion, the bloody hanger-on, the servant) an open-handed smack across the face, hearing Moon whine in surprise.

The slap has worked him up. A fizz of adrenalin courses through him. He retraces his route, arriving back at the yard. Again he scours the skies. No sign, none, not a single bird. The phone, there must be a number, someone could find them. Even if they were to drive round themselves, he and Wik, they could call everyone in a hundred miles. There's a directory for this area . . .

Pacing around the yard, kneeling every now and again to commiserate with Moon, he hunts for a sight of anything flying through the range of light cast by the yard's halogens.

The only ones which might survive are the piping plovers – rare, but from this eastern seaboard.

He can't trust his memory.

Four

BUDDY MAZE IS squaring up to a bellyful: cactus soup, then rabbit sticks in peanut sauce to go on with, followed by country-cure ham steaks with pineapple and sweet fruit and cinnamon gravy, hash potatoes, grilled tomatoes topped with basil, hot baby cucumbers, followed by three chocolate buffalos and then coffees and a cigar. The last thing to be set in front of him is a three-hundred-year-old brandy floating in the bottom of a glass as big as a fishbowl.

Opposite him is a woman who is a woman – perhaps. He cannot be quite sure. It's not just the short hair and the incongruous combat fatigues, it's her skin's grain – distinctly masculine. The slope of her chest gives nothing away because she's thin. She eats like a man: it's necessary (a job of work) to eat, not an entertainment, nor a problem, and she smokes like a rig. A professor in medicine, but she's got a heavy enough habit to take the pack with her when she goes to the restrooms?

'So!' he cries. The conversation between himself and this Professor Sage Tinkler so far hasn't matched up, any attempted salvo by either of them has shot wide. They've meandered through several topics, but Buddy was into his food, he marked mostly the diminishing patterns of individual meats, sauces and vegetables, trying to orchestrate it so the last forkful included the platters' complete variety. 'Down to business.'

'OK.' The Professor looks at him just as stolidly as before – he was expecting her to be relieved or excited. But she acts just the same as the whole time they've sat here, like she's been in a fight and won.

'Of course, you'll have guessed I want you to come work at La Paz.'

She nods assent.

Buddy Maze is reaching out to a further horizon now. Because he could walk through Mexico City and idly but realistically consider buying at once every building he walks past (he's more seriously thinking of putting in an offer for the airport), he has the sensation that he's grown bigger: his step shakes the pavement, the lobes of his ears flap like dewlaps, his view has risen to a point from which he can look down on these buildings, this city, the country, continent and world, from which vantage an ordinary human purchase (food, carpet cleaner, second-hand car, bungalow) seems unbelievably mysterious: that people should struggle, or even have to do such things? And from this high point he can reach much further – it delights him that he can lift a phone and reel in this woman.

'OK, run your stuff past me. What you've done? Just shorthand.'

'You already know.'

'I know some. But I want to hear it from you, get a handle on what sort of person you are.'

This glib utterance satisfies him as would (he imagines) the perfect delivery of a tennis serve – not that he's sporting, his game is greed, everyone an opponent but no one threatening him currently.

Professor Sage Tinkler asks (her slow look with no lights on inside), 'Starting where?'

Buddy Maze feels genial. 'Wherever you like. How'd you get interested in this stuff you been doing?'

She should be courting him more, what with the amount of money she was asking. Her matter-of-fact look, her flat dark pupils, her mere tolerance of him, is unnerving. How did such a skinny woman do so much?

She says, 'I got interested when I was a kid. Pulling cars to bits and putting them back together.'

'You had brothers, huh?' Buddy Maze is pleased with this observation.

'No.'

He looks shocked. 'OK! You were one of these tough girls.'

'Tough enough.'

'How did cars get to medicine?'

'Medicine is the same as cars. It's still fixing things. Except it's a human body instead of a V8. It's all pipes and tubes, intake and emissions? An engine has a heart, a pair of lungs. Or four lungs or six lungs. A blood supply, a fuel line, a waste system. An engine needs to be kept at a certain temperature. It's exactly the same. It's all fix-it technology.'

'So I'll be a Cadillac, sort of, I dig . . .' Buddy Maze shrugs and gives an admiring smile.

Professor Tinkler adds, 'But seeing as there's no money in motors, I went into medicine.'

'OK.'

'Did a thesis on the psychology of intensive care.'

'Seems it got to be a famous little thesis, that one, although no one like me, no one in real life ever got to hear of it.'

She studies him carefully before continuing. 'Spent the war

89

years in emergency fieldwork. Saving lives from about as bad trauma-injuries as anyone gets to see.'

'Valuable work on any scoreboard.'

'Next three years in the Methuselah Clinic, Switzerland.'

'I read about it of course, on your cure-ik-you-lum vee-tie.'

'Now I'm . . . freelance.' She lifts a tiny hand – the cigarette is almost as big as one of the fingers holding it.

Buddy Maze leans forward as though there's something suspicious about that word. 'Freelance?'

'Yes.'

'But not free, eh? A hahaha! Not free, exactly, I bet!' He weeps with laughter.

'No,' replies Professor Sage Tinkler, 'not free.'

Buddy Maze recovers. He slots his nose into the top of the brandy glass and waits for a while before sipping, breathing in the pungent fumes. Each breath costs, he reminds himself, inhaling deeply.

'Now,' he continues, 'that's just writing on a page, though, ain't it? Impressive: the top grades, the whatsit, the thesis on lots of caring, the war work – on both sides, I hear, for Chrissake, you can't get more impartial than that – the Methuselah Clinic I wanted to get to know a little more about later, uh, so on. Yeah, impressive.'

'Thank you.'

'But I kinda need to know about you – as a person. Now how about I tell you what I want exactly?'

'OK.'

Buddy Maze sniffs, waiting for a build-up in the amount of sincerity he can put into this.

'I have someone very dear to me,' he begins, 'an old guy who's more to me than any man, more to me than my whole

90

family put together. But . . . he is old, there's no getting round that. He's . . . just . . . old!'

He sighs and looks up at her. 'I'm sure I don't have to tell you who that man is.'

'No, you don't.'

'You heard about him.'

'I know him.'

'Huh!'

'I did a bone-marrow harvest for him back a while.'

'Hell no, it's a small world up there at the top of your tree.'

Buddy marks time. The food is well packed in his stomach. The brandy's doing its job, making him a good man, the sort of man he wants to be. Maybe he'll pay for this meal, maybe not. The fun of being explosively rich is, so many people want to get a hook into you that you end up not having to pay for anything much. It costs less being rich than it does being poor.

But there is this problem of reading the woman in front of him. There's rumours, and there's what she's told him, but he's not yet getting a sure enough hang of her.

So Buddy Maze adds, with a touch of urgency, 'Professor, it's simple, I just want him to get the best there is. You are the best.'

She seems to have ignored his plea, because she starts on a different tack. She says, 'What was it I heard, a one-hundred-and-thirty-year gifting programme?'

The words ring in his ears.

She adds, 'Kind of too long, for a man gone seventy.'

Buddy slides his tongue over his gums, spreading the astringent brandy to those musty parts of his mouth which can get forgotten about.

He is enlivened.

'So you heard about that?'

'Yup.'

'Read it in the press?'

'Who hasn't? Most famous gifting programme of all time.'

Having already worked out her possible deal a move or two ahead, seeing through the legal wrapping of this thing, Professor Tinkler suspects that when Ambelin dies, what's bequeathed, whatever's his legacy, will supersede the gifting programme.

To confirm, she states flatly, 'I take it there's no completion clause.'

Some woman.

Buddy sinks into a slow, careful attitude. He considers things, and concludes that he wanted, anyway, to get to this level.

He speaks then in a moderately interested, friendly voice, as though he's telling a story of someone far away from either of them.

'You know, I heard some stuff, in the press and whatnot. Kind of odd rumours. In 1972 there was this ancient war criminal? Got his life saved by a woman calling herself Doctor Jameson, so they said. And back awhile a Turkish village, called Jakarti or somethin', is discovered, and half the residents kind of only have one eye. And most of 'em have had a kidney or some part of their stomach or intestine tubes removed. Hell, funny thing is, they all got Mickey Mouse watches and new shoes. The sicker they are the more watches and shoes they own. And guess what, that's just the ones that are still living. There was rumours that a certain clinic was owned and run by a white woman near by, with all white patients, but no one found anything. And just back a year, a woman was about to be prosecuted for the illegal supply of *cadavers*? Case got overthrown for some pretty goddam mysterious reasons.'

She faces this with absolute calm. 'So we understand each other.' She stubs her cigarette out.

'I guess so,' Buddy maze settles it with a smile.

'I know so.'

'Well,' replies Buddy, cheerfully, 'so now I can real happily tell you there's no completion clause.'

'Have you seen his will?'

Buddy shakes his head. 'Uh-uh. Not allowed. All I know is – it's old, from way back, the '70s. So it's kinda unlikely I'm in it.'

'He might be about to change it.'

'He might be. But I'm not gonna ask him to do so. I might be able to turn him around to thinkin' about it and so on. But that's a game best played real slow. So the deal is, until I'm in there with my name down on that bit of paper, I want you around.' He leans forward. 'Also, you should understand what type of guy we're dealin' with. If you showed Ambelin Sayers a dollar bill he maybe wouldn't, actually, you know, recognise what it was. He has a team of guys, lawyers and so on who do all his stuff, who buy his fuckin' toilet paper practically. It wouldn't surprise me if he's forgotten he ever made a will or even that such a thing exists? He gives an order, sure, but these lawyer guys do it how they think best, they're watchin' for him, we're dealin' with those guys too and they're some smart cookies.'

Sage Tinkler says, 'OK. So, now I have a question.'

'Shoot.'

She asks, 'Can you afford me?'

He won't show excitement. He recalls going to buy a car with his dad, as a football-shaped boy, and getting keener the more he circled this car, and his father angry afterwards because he'd been unable to get the price lower, blaming the boy's enthusiasm as affecting the negotiation.

So he says, 'That depends.'

She insists, 'I'll want to do research. I'm not going to sit around looking after one guy if there's nothing much wrong with him. Can you afford equipment and a team of four? My lab, an ICU and four extra salaries, that is.'

Buddy finds his options closing. Having straightened up, now he has to have her on his side, she can't be on the loose . . . What the hell?

He says, 'Honey, you do your job, and I can afford to pay for your white mice.'

He adds, 'But you fail, and we both go down.'

Her first smile to him comes now. 'Well . . . as long as we go down together.'

So he laughs, grandly, with maximum confidence. 'Here,' he says, leaning across to pick up her packet of cigarettes, 'have one of mine.'

SERIOUS RESPONSIBILITY is new to Arthur Cinsaretti. His first wife was older than him and had died leaving his ironing folded and not only enough money to pay for someone but the someone too: a loose-lipped old Georgian lady had been identified and hired during the cancerous period preceding her death. Since he's had to take care of his own house, though, Arthur has faced up to it with earnest common sense, which attribute, he has frequently argued, is equivalent to hedonism because after all if you want your food on time, your Diet Coke sprinkled with fresh mint, your lawn edges trimmed, the sheets crisp, if you want these pleasures then it's only sensical organisation that will get them for you.

With the slender, hard-plastic wheel of the Cheetah V12 running through the light grip of both hands set correctly at the ten-to-two position, inviting dizziness if he looks at the instrument panel through the inner chrome-plated circle (pressure on which activates the horn), turning a cluster of outward spokes all glistering in the sun, like this Arthur serenely drives his future wife (he checks often whether or not her knees are covered) back to the Monsoon Motel whither she moved, after her tenants arrived. All this is so that he, Arthur Cinsaretti, can meet her son TJ.

'TJ . . . this is Mr Cinsaretti.'

Amie is speaking to her son from the passenger seat of the Cheetah, now majestically stationed outside their motel rooms. Mr Cinsaretti gets out of the car but for some reason Amie stays put, although her door is open. She is fully made up and has been running dry for two days.

TJ registers Mr Cinsaretti. The real detail of the man confounds and (remarkably quickly) replaces the picture he's made in his head. He sees immediately, at a stroke, that Arthur is a short man with a straight back and a bald pate fringed with thin brown hair, looking expensive and unafraid.

Arthur calls, 'TJ . . . I've heard many good things about you.' He gives a positive handshake.

TJ, fleetingly worried that his hand is clammy from holding the beer can, says, 'Actually, sir, I'm not called TJ any more. My name's Lambent.'

'Lambent?' asks Arthur Cinsaretti, 'I never heard of the name Lambent.'

'It's not so much a name.'

'What is it?'

'A word.'

Still cheerful, Arthur replies, 'I ain't heard of no word called Lambent either.'

TJ admits, 'It means quietly brilliant.'

'Uh-uh.'

Unabashed, Mr Cinsaretti is moving round to close the drophead roof of the Cheetah and TJ understands why his mother has stayed sitting in the car: it's her job to do up the clips. So now she can get out.

'He's a zero,' TJ mutters, low enough so only she can hear.

Amie sticks her tongue out at her son.

She feels small and (thankfully) encased in protective layers painfully beaten out, made of behaviour: this is her self for Arthur, there's another for TJ, furthest within is her small, weak, sorrowful soul, thirsty for any tranquillant, curling its toes, staring at the space where Ambelin, or someone like him, should be. She blames in turn *him*, herself, the world, timing, luck, fate. All other men, even harmless Arthur, are just so many hands coming from various directions towards her, she having to pick them off and cast them away. TJ, however, standing there, cheeking her at the moment, is a mascot, a different, smaller but more distilled version of the time of her life with Ambelin. To spy TJ (especially now he is growing tall enough, filling towards a correctly proportioned body) wins her on occasions an immediate memoir of his father; TJ taking a particular pose or unconsciously affecting a recognisable gesture making it stronger in the same way that a precise smell can let in a sudden backdraught of time, more certainly experienced, even, than before – and this won't allow her to escape from the tyranny of his remembrance, even if she should want to. TJ's mind-workings also add to the play of shadow on her recollections of Ambelin because she observes the way he can be concentrating hard on one thing, focused earnestly enough to be destructive (a dismantled TV set once got strewn across his room, slowly, carefully, exploded by his intensive curiosity), when, of a sudden, he will make a logical but wildly lateral leap and fix on something else (in that instance it was transvestism and he's been wearing long hair for a year). Her amusement at this copied trait of character in TJ has a tang of resentment in it because Ambelin, after his initial devouring of her seventeen years ago, made just such a leap from a full-time admiration of her to concentrate instead on designing a perfectly shaped bra for the women of America – when he stopped and looked round to find her, she'd already run.

'You guys known each other long?' TJ asks Arthur, impressed at the routine with the car roof.

His mother replies, 'Mr Cinsaretti has been a friend long enough for me to know he will be a good influence on you, TJ.'

'Uh-huh.'

'You've not had the discipline of a father. It will do you good to learn from Mr . . . from Arthur. I make no secret of the fact that I admire him and consider him to be a good lesson for you.'

Why does his mother put on this funny voice with men?

'I'm real thankful, Mom,' replies TJ as they lead the way inside.

Mr Cinsaretti has lit his cigarette and now follows them into room 171. He plants himself squarely on one leg, the cigarette held like a pen, squinting at TJ's beer can. 'TJ . . . I mean – son, I wouldn't start drinking alcohol if I were you.'

TJ listens, amazed.

Arthur continues, confidently, 'It's something I learnt when I was a bit older than you, but hell I wish someone had got round to teaching me earlier. See, I used to play pool, used to drink, used to gamble. Fact is you oughta know I once reached the final of the Wichihati All-State Winners Play-off and backed myself to the hilt.' He leans forward. 'And won' (ridiculously, he leans forward further), 'and drunk myself so stupid I lost it straightaways at crap.' He plants himself back to a balanced pose. 'I heard the Lord that night. A strange ranting sound. And in the gutter I had my hands clapped over my ears in fear of the Lord. Since that day I have not touched a drop nor have I played pool, never play now, not ever. I can watch, teach a little maybe. Never play.'

He looks thoughtful.

'The Lord was angry, damned angry, and I'm not afraid to confess it scared me.'

'There's nothing worse than drink.' This was from his mother.

'That's true, I suppose it is bad,' replies TJ.

His mother's gaze is on him, but empty of expression. 'Drink is the devil's water,' she adds, still deadpan.

'OK, so I'll stop too.' TJ pours his own half-empty can down the drain in the kitchenette.

Arthur calls, 'Iced coffee is all I look at, an' that's all I'd have anyone else look at.'

He adds, 'Apart from your mother, I'd have everyone look at her. Beauty ain't harmed a soul ever.'

AMBELIN SAYERS ROAMS the bijou passenger lounge of the twin-jet aircraft; he is the only one in there, a sole traveller in the white mileage of this sky, in the Corporation plane which used to be an air-taxi for him during former times, fuelled for transglobal destinations, chasing down or running from the world's continual lip service to the sun. The crown of his head is an inch lower (sunk in disbelief) under the top side of the scooped-out alloy. He can take four paces sideways, twelve back and forth. He has no luggage because, fearful of what he found was happening in what he's come to know must be the seat of human agitation, the sternum, he immediately ran, after one act: telephoning Buddy Maze in Mexico to say he was on his way.

He stoops to peer from a window. Clouds are spun out in rows. He is trapped in a winged bullet flying thirty thousand feet up, nothing but air and coldness and ribs of moisture between him and the ground. He's an old, fading dot on a radar screen, breasting the newly changed map of the world, fractured by the time zones he's going through.

Feather-light controls guarantee a rarefied choice of music, and he settles marginally now that the suck of the engines is reduced to the merest hush underneath the lone call of a Welsh boy, recorded in a Venetian church four years before, singing from a score composed three hundred years earlier, Purcell's 'Ode to St Cecilia' perfectly reproduced now in a pressurised cabin aimed through thin air.

He is in sadness.

Standing at full height, his gaze set absent-mindedly for

half-way to the horizon, Ambelin mouths the words, making no sound, not even a whisper, because to do so would spoil the boy's voice, truer, as it is, than his ever will be.

Moon is pressed to the floor – under a seat. Her flanks are pumping, slowly. She will remain this way, petrified. It's difficult to get her on a plane – he has to cajole her at length before she'll embark and her back legs buckled with fear as she climbed the steps.

He supposes that this might be a facility offered only to people with his count of years: he can relive his infancy, and it was watching the check of his father's jacket approaching, the pattern in the hound's-tooth cloth bewitching his new sight and obscuring the sense of a person within, then, as it drew closer still, working on him maybe like a gyroscopic mechanism, throwing his unpractised focus and causing him a confusing, giddy pain (perhaps his first) that seems to him to be proof he's not good at people coming close? His terrible mistake in the aviary has shocked him in this way mysteriously: he can't face Wik Slavery, not in person, although his friend is of course like a mote floating for ever in the play of his sight. Close his eyes and it's there, that face . . . before running for the airport he suffered revulsion at the sight of the back of Wik Slavery's neck – he walked past twice and saw the line of his haircut parallel to the back of the chair and on both occasions he felt a shameful instinct towards his friend – his failure has made him bitter, and his wish to avoid Wik comes of shame. His senile, oldster's blunder of somehow loosing all the cages is an odious memory. Words of self-accusation drop like poison. If he ever smiles again it will be like a cut to kill good humour.

Working himself up, Ambelin Sayers angles slowly around

the lounge of the jet like a housefly, humming away in persistent humiliation. He bumps his heart, which is sticking against the wall of his chest. Grief, he's going too fast, too high. He will break up. Covered in wrinkles, he resembles a cartoon when all the lines move and reassemble themselves, anger mapping his face, truly fierce terrain. His hands are clenched; he realises he's been shouting.

Moon's out from her place; her snout is in one of his hands. He drops to her level, his knees cracking. She gives a sudden hop and puts her forelegs up on their old station – his shoulders – and he's cooing, calming her. She's quick to return to her place when he stands.

He holds his nose, experimenting with pressure. His ears feel lanced by thin pain.

Does he have no more of the famous Sayers steel left in his nerves? Old rope in comparison. What's happened? He could weld guys together with anger in times gone. The business! The snap and play of those days!

A grief-note bursts from him.

The stewardess comes and cleans him up. Some disgusting event down his front – he missed it but something must have happened because here she is smiling and wiping him down.

As the jet, minutely, sharpened by the sun's blades, traverses the limitless cloud (floating in the earth's blue lung), Ambelin meanders on, picking over the deep past: ideas and judgements spiced with the odd sensation such as the graze of his father's beard. This track (old, familiar) saves him from guilt.

He feels a lost man.

How did he loose those cages?

For two hours he engages himself in an experiment: taking a

pen and paper (both crested 'Sayers' – often he thinks each printing of the name has lost him a microscopic portion of his self; this is him running out), he writes down everything he does. He chooses to peer from a window, to summon the hostess and request a glass of milk, to inspect himself in the mirror (stooping in the miniature toilet cubicle and dragging at his skin which is drying out badly in the enforced atmosphere of the plane), and he notes each action. Later, perhaps tomorrow, he will test himself by attempting to recall what he's done and checking it against the list. He dreads it may prove to be the flight, or the test itself, then his name, his existence, that he will forget.

He has to sit now; the hostess fastens a buckle across his lap. Moon is pinning herself down under her chair, even her tail is flattened to the floor.

The nerve-racking sounds begin: dramatic variations in engine pitch and the graunch of the landing-gear lowering.

Touchdown. A skating – and then the reverse thrust. Safety. Some fears melt away, so others are distilled – but he pathetically hopes for a reduction.

Moon scrambles for the exit. He can hear the clatter of her claws on the metal.

At the top of the steps he is amazed. Flashing, blasted by heat, in a race, incongruously, with the yellow toilet-services truck, a Viper V8 pick-up is haring over the pavement with (as he can make out when it dives to a halt beneath him) an American flag strung from fender to fender. Ambelin, standing there, stuck to the clothes that he's worn for three days now, worked over by injustice, mourning his birds, scared for his future, loves it to death when the giant torso of Buddy Maze bowls out of the driver's side of the Viper, when the door gets slammed so hard it makes the vehicle rock sideways on its wishbones, when Buddy stands there at the bottom of the steps, legs braced, arms outstretched, and that grin comes, and he shouts with rude lack of affectation, 'Ambelin, my old buddy!'

Ambelin takes the steps one at a time (he used to be able to trot down), excitement rising, a relief tide. He wants to embrace his friend but he's too tall, it would look wrong.

Mixed with kerosene from the jet engines Ambelin (as he shakes Buddy Maze's hand) smells comforting foodstuffs: spice and frying-grease.

It takes three hours to La.Paz: home. Ambelin doesn't mind the broken road or the pull of the corners, he doesn't mind anything. Moon sits beside him in the Viper like a human. (Soon she will solve the big mystery and learn to speak to Ambelin, she's on the cusp of that achievement, even now she believes she can get through with one or two messages so consequently has sympathy for Ambelin's attempts to speak to her – and Ambelin is no cleverer than she is. They are on either side of a language, both of them anxious to cross over.)

After a while he's not listening to Buddy Maze so much, and it being his way, Ambelin continues obsessively on the line of remembering his life. When, for instance, was the first time he had the recurring dream of his teeth being unbolted and laid out on a workbench . . .?

Turning in through the gates at the beginning of the three-mile driveway to La Paz, Ambelin sees activity: a gang surrounding smoking vats of asphalt on the backs of the parked-up flatbed trucks. He exclaims, 'Pavement!'

'Sure!'

'My jaw shakes goin' down here.'

103

'One of the first things I started, pavement on the drive,' answers Buddy Maze.

Once they've taken the third steep curve, Ambelin's keen for a first sighting of his ocean home – it will be the roof at the back of the house and a white corner. As they draw closer he's hungry for any sign of change. 'New deck?'

'Yeah, had to put a sundeck in. Not the same otherwise, even if it does have to be netted up.'

'What else?'

'Oh I got loads of plans. You'll see.' They are out of the Viper now, on the way in, Ambelin shading his eyes, needing sunglasses, Buddy popping a Baby Doll and thumbing the spent wrapper into a back pocket of his shorts. 'Yeah, the sundeck,' he says, thumping an upright with the heel of his hand. 'No hangin' about!'

Ambelin feels a lurch of anxiety: Wik Slavery. What did that mean? He has his list in the pocket of his coat. Where's his coat? Instructing himself not to fret, he looks forward to lying down in a bed of warm sand and allowing the sun to stroke him for hours on end. He has a place for doing that here.

Buddy Maze rolls indoors, Ambelin follows. It's quiet and cool – the plainness of the outside gives way to an interior splendour, how the Arabs do it. To one side of the tiled hallway stand two chairs. With the casual grace of a good parent Buddy Maze guides Ambelin over and seats him, then sits himself, so they wait like potentates until two women appear with bowls of tepid water.

Buddy Maze always looks down because the woman kneeling has got a bust as hefty as a normal woman's ass. She takes his sandals off and begins to wash his feet.

'Good, ain't it?'

'I like ritual.' Ambelin's heart skids, banging in its hollow. He's worried about arterial hypertension and remembers the doctor's advice: keep breathing evenly when excited. His large vessels, even, feel too small for this. Fatigue is loaded on top of him . . . a nerve in his elbow won't allow him to lock his arm open so it lies like a broken stick in his lap. But there's this woman washing his feet! The water is warm. It itches where the surface tension holds his ankles. He feels the soapy fingers on and around his feet; like eels they worm between the toes.

Moon waits, standing adrift in the middle of the hall.

Buddy Maze says, 'It's a custom ought to be done more often between folks familiar with each other.'

'You're not wrong,' Ambelin agrees. He too gazes down on his woman's breasts rolling against each other – his old body, his old thoughts and memories are all delighted. Feeling the same rise in emotion as before accepting a prize or delivering an achievement to the American public, he says, 'Will be a keepsake event, no mistake, an' I thank you from top to toe.'

'Top to toe, hahaha, top to toe,' exclaims Buddy Maze, lifting a foot from the bowl.

He adds, 'It's simple things ain't it, that stay reliable on you. Like good eats. Like a knowledgeable woman. Like a handshake. Like a washin' of your feet in this parched land. Rill simple things. Enjoy.'

The towelling is careful and thorough.

They both stand up together. Ambelin enjoys the bump against Buddy Maze's stomach and the hand that comes out to save him from falling back in the chair.

'House slippers right there.'

'Uh-huh.'

Buddy Maze leads him on a fat-hipped roll. 'Oceanside rooms for you, of course,' he says. 'The wife and I are further along – an' you're welcome anytime, but, you got all you need here if you want to be on your lonesome.'

Buddy Maze holds one hand against the small of the older man's back and guides him along.

The ex-Chairman of the Sayers Corporation is happy, beaten with this storm of attention. His teeth are tight, in place. He can smell mustard from somewhere.

Buddy says, 'This is you.' They walk in and Buddy Maze starts pointing. 'Rest room, closet, bed, TV and stereo stuff, remotes somewhere, lounge through there, bell-pull here, help-alarm, kitchen, food 'n' all, should you not want to bother with us. And here, look, right, I had the guys round and they worked all night to drop this 'splay window in here – see? The ocean. You sit up in bed, and you see the fuckin' ocean. What d'you think?'

Old man Sayers stands in the middle of the room; turns this way and that. All his stuff, his collection of glass manuscripts, his animal masks, his books, every inch of the wallspace is crowded with his things.

'You do this?'

'Yup. Like it?'

Ambelin lifts his hands, claps twice and drops them. He shakes his head. 'Wonderful.'

He feels the healthy chill of Moon's nose again delivered into the palm of his hand; he takes hold of the mutt's snout and squeezes it gently. Moon stays put, trusting him.

Ambelin asks, 'And we can make plans, huh?'

'Yeah!' Buddy Maze waves a hand like he's indicating them all laid out. 'We can make plans!'

'Hey, you like chess?'

'Love it.'

'We can play.'

'Sure can,' replies Buddy.

He adds, as a last thing before leaving, 'Now, I'll let you rest up – but you treat this like what it is, your home, OK?'

TJ'S TOO WEARY to ask what town this is, what road they're on. Only Arthur bothers with the route. Towards 'Oregon'. It's a sad name. The last half echoes, 'gone . . .'

They've already made two pool stops, this is the third.

Leading TJ up five concrete steps into what appears to be (from the outside) a school hall, Arthur Cinsaretti proclaims, 'You get taught by me, you'll be winning by a year's time.'

The inside of the building belies its frontage – within are sixteen full-size pitches floating (you can't see their undersides) under oblong light-baths hung low over the tables, the chains disappearing quickly towards an invisible ceiling. TJ follows Arthur, who is negotiating the avenues and smaller roads between the tables towards the mini-bar in the corner, which houses a fat man on a stool eating the two-meat filling from a submarine in one hand, watching their approach and turning the pages of a copy of *NationHood* magazine opened over his knees. Arthur snaps a ten-dollar bill, twists it and, using this crucial key into the event, comes back with a rack of balls and two sodas.

Being daytime, only one other table is busy; the users, a man and a woman, dip alternately to address the white. Arthur chooses the pitch next to theirs.

When TJ goes to pick a cue from the stall, Arthur waves him away making a tutting noise, claiming, 'They'll all be outa true. You can use mine.'

He takes off his tie and jacket, unsheaths his cue and chalks the tip, all in a flurry, twice checking the players on the other table and talking more quickly than before.

'Lesson number one, it's a game of straight lines, is all, intersecting straight lines and the transfer of kinetic energy. But first straight lines.'

TJ is left standing, hands in pockets, thinking how Arthur's ring of hair looks devilish. TJ's recent fascination with transvestite murderers might lead him to see the worst in people, currently, but even offsetting this, he thinks his mother's new boyfriend must have been overcooked at some stage.

Arthur puts the chalk in the middle of the rubber at one end, corrals the white with his cue and shepherds it to the other end.

He says, glibly, 'The straight aim is the name of the game,' sets the white near a corner pocket, rolling it with two neatly joined fingers to position it . . . precisely, and hardly pausing to aim sends it down the table to strike the rubber fronted by the chalk, the ball losing impetus now, strolling back up the table to disappear neatly into the corner pocket.

'Try for that,' says Arthur; 'have one shot without me saying anything and let's see what your natural stroke's like.'

TJ pulls his hands free, ready to oblige, but (mysteriously) Arthur's moving on too fast and forgets to hand him the cue, instead standing with it upended on his foot, both hands encircling the slim end in front of him, looking wistfully out towards where the man and the woman are playing, lifting his toe occasionally to feel the wood slide against the inside of his knuckle.

TJ wonders how far Arthur has got with his mother. Have her arms sealed around his neck, ever? Don't mind it, he commands himself, and the worry that he wants to kill Arthur subsides. After all he's not interested in murder (unlike the TVs), only in clever crime.

Arthur is shouting now. 'OK do this.' He hurries to retrieve the white from the trap and places it against one side. 'Let's go. Trick shot.' He cues it down the line, into the mouth of the corner, miraculously sending the ball running out along the bottom-most end, still close on the edge, having bounced twice off the curved rubber in the pocket. As a final grace it pops down at the next corner.

Arthur calls to the players on the next table who are moving through the choreography of an often-practised game – 'Hey, do that and you'll be half-way good as me.' They pause to look at him, otherwise their reaction is disappointing.

Arthur murmurs something.

TJ finds the wall and settles into a serious lean. He might even sit down during his pool lesson. He watches Arthur draw a twenty-dollar bill from the clip in his back pocket.

'You keep your money in your pocket, son,' Arthur advises TJ as he passes to where the other two are playing, holding his cue over his shoulder as though it were a rifle. TJ can see the twenty woven between his fingers, held like a flag against his chest as he earnestly watches their play. When the last solid goes down Arthur lets his cue slip and drums the end on the floor in appreciation.

The man, who's just won a try at the black, forgets the table for now and comes to confront Arthur. 'Say . . .'

'Arthur Cinsaretti, Wichihati All-State Players Champion, pleased to meet you.'

The other man ignores the introduction, Arthur's extended hand, the twenty woven between the fingers. He carries on from where he left off. 'I'm not all the way sure what's happening here, but me and my friend, we're just finishing up our little game, then we're moving on? Neither one of us wants . . . anything. So, can I ask you to quieten, huh?'

'Sure, sure. I'm just watching, is all.'

'Please don't.'

'Right, OK.' Arthur is backing away. 'I respect that. I understand what you're saying.'

When the man returns to his game Arthur lingers as close as he dares, waiting to refuel with self-respect; the nearer he can stay to their table, and the longer, the more dignity he might retrieve.

TJ decides to say he's not up to playing; maybe he'll go back to the motel.

Arthur replies, 'Sure, son. Sure.'

Left alone, Arthur tries to shrug off any loss of comfort. He has a rack of balls. Alternating between solids and stripes, he plays himself.

MEXICO CITY. From the airport, driving to the unknown, Wik Slavery is worried, out of place. Squinting through the cab window, he notices that no one looks like him, there's none of him about.

Momentarily checked at a light, he sees a scruff walking towards him, slavering at an ice-cream. The man dips his head to check the interior of the cab. Wik looks away, but the greaseball keeps on coming and throws his ice-cream at the window. Wik exclaims and recoils. The man walks carelessly hard into the side of the cab, slamming it with the palms of his hands and with his boots; the cab driver swears and takes off, breaking the red.

Later on in the journey, Wik is worried enough about the route to rap on the partition separating him from the rude black curls massed on the back of the taxi driver's head. The latter feels behind him for the handle, slips back the scratched plexiglas panel and leans an ear back, still keeping his eye on the traffic heaving and flashing in front of him.

'Er . . . *¿Está seguro . . .?*' Wik doesn't know enough Spanish for this so instead he pokes the slip of paper through the partition and shouts, 'Are you sure this is where we're going?'

The driver takes the paper, consults it two or three times in between steering the car, then hands it back.

'Hotel Candida,' he confirms. '*Está allá*. Iz there.' He makes a victory sign. 'Two kilometres.'

As he leans back Wik catches a speculative look from a pair of black eyes condensed and aimed at him, bounced off the rear-view mirror.

He feels the nausea of extreme poverty around him, and closing.

The Hotel Candida looks blasted by dirt and gunfire, although everything is peaceable enough. Wik Slavery fears his own conspicuousness even more than the dark slot of the hotel's mouth, so, just to hide his white sneakers, slacks and shirt from people who might think it worthwhile to get anything any way they can, he goes in. Hadn't there been something in a newspaper about shirt-murders? How they

111

stabbed the inside of your thigh to save spoiling certain fashionable marks of shirt? He shudders.

Safe off the street he again checks: his bag, yes. Money? Yes. Passport? He pats his pockets. Passport missing? He disbelieves, makes a flurried search. It is the truth. His passport is gone.

He checks the road outside. No sign of the taxi. The whole place is seething with other, bashed-up cars. He curses. A sudden vulnerability disturbs him. No passport. He finds himself in sympathy with a wrecked man who is droning out a plaintive chant over on the other side of the road, his face burnt up by the sun but none the less angled straight at it, eyes closed.

He will need the Consul, he will have to hang around, fill in forms. He'll need another photograph of himself (he remembers his front cover of *NationHood*).

Can he call the embassy from Buddy Maze's room? Inside the foyer he is faced by what looks like a prison cell – a woman is sitting behind steel bars in a booth barely big enough for her to turn in. But it's not to lock her in, it's to keep others *out*. Away from the money.

She smiles mechanically but with radical stretching of her lips.

She says his name! The accent is ridiculous but he's almost sure that was his name?

Letting herself out of her cage, she begins to talk, speaking in a profusion of clacking sounds that he can't understand. He supposes that he is meant to follow her as she walks off.

Sordid here. He feels safer because she's leading him.

He remembers a conversation, his therapist starting it, saying to him, 'You have no male friends?'

'I do.'

'Don't do a denial on me this early on in a session that costs you more than it takes to feed an Ethiopian family for a year, Wik.'

'OK, I don't have male friends, so what?'

'Suspicious, huh?'

'What?'

'Don't you think it's suspicious, that you don't have male friends?'

'No.'

'OK, you're the boss. It's not strange at all.'

As they rise he glimpses on every level verandahs running around an inner courtyard. Washing is strung on cords, making random patterns along the walkways. Are the clothes so clean, or is it because the hotel is dirty? By the time he's reached the third level he's worked out that it's the bleaching effect of sunlight.

The woman leading him dabs a finger at a doorway and operates her mechanical mouth again, holding out a hand. It takes him too long to find any bills but her comfortless smile remains engaged until she's got the cash and measured its value; he spots the smile vanishing as she turns away.

Buddy Maze answers the door wearing a robe, chewing a triplemint, tequila in hand. He looks with care into Wik Slavery's face. Adopting a quizzical expression, he shouts, 'Hey, María, Bonita, Barbarama, whatever your name is.'

Wik yawns.

Buddy smiles. 'Hey, hey, c'mon, move your pussy! Manuela! What's your name!'

A girl appears. Buddy is still studying Wik's face. 'You can go now. ¡Vaya! ¡Fuera!'

113

The girl slips past them.

'So, Wik, thanks for coming. Good to see you lookin' well 'n' up here. Because I want to help, you know?'

Wik accepts this, but he's wanting to deal with his missing passport first.

Buddy continues, 'I spoke to Ambelin, of course, about why he ran off from yours. Just dropped it in, made light of it. But you know how he is when he wants to avoid something? It's like he's not *there* on that subject. It simply doesn't go in. He's on a different ride, it's like he's finished with it, like he's . . . forgotten.'

Now Buddy Maze wanders, collecting a tumbler, pouring. Wik gets offered something in the cheap kitchen glass.

Wik says, 'Just before we go on, can I make a call? My passport's been stolen.'

Buddy Maze swings round to face him square on. His knees buckle; he's bending like a Sumo wrestler. 'Goddam, no, your passport?' He sounds incredulous. Then he straightens. His mouth stays open.

Wik says, 'I'd better phone as soon as possible. I kind of need it, obviously.'

Buddy spreads his hands. 'You can try, sure.'

Wik lifts the receiver and hears nothing. 'The line's down?'

'You bet.' Buddy chuckles. 'They say phones in every room but they don't say nothing about no plugs on the wall. Not to worry. We'll get your call in, get you some temporary ID.'

Then Buddy asks, 'Bring anyone with you?'

'No.'

'Anyone know you're here?'

'No.'

Buddy explains, 'I'm not all the way sure Ambelin would

114

approve of us talking without him being here, with us that is, so it's why I'm making kind of a fuss over secrecy. But that's not to say I'm droppin' you for him, not in any way. What I want is what we had to start, all three of us happy, Ambelin, me, you?'

'Sure. That's all I want.'

Buddy Maze purses his lips and sighs. Planting himself on a chair, he says with absolute confidence, 'I'm sure we can do something.'

Wik feels small. Buddy is staring at him, switching his gaze from one part of him to another, which is unnerving. The man's stillness and this flicking of his eyes. He again sees the ice-cream hitting the window inches from his face. An unhinged venom, that was. He shudders; the alcohol in his mouth. He swallows more tequila fast to cover himself.

'OK.' Buddy takes off from the chair and settles on another closer by. His voice is sympathetic. 'Now let's get you and this Ambelin problem sorted.' He clunks the bottle against their tumblers. The tequila has a powerful smell and Buddy advises Wik, pointing at the glass, 'Chuck it in, shouldn't do it any other way. Toss it to the back of your throat.'

He adds, 'So. What to do, huh?'

'I don't know. What's best?' Wik Slavery sits, watching the other man snatch the label off a new pair of socks.

'Look at this,' exclaims Buddy Maze, suddenly. He takes a cigarette butt from the ashtray and relights it, squinting.

'Gimme your shirt.'

He moves next to Wik Slavery on the settle. Pegging the cigarette in the corner of his mouth, he takes hold of a piece of Wik's shirt, putting one hand underneath the cloth and drilling it with his thumb until there's a small well of cloth enclosed by

115

his fingers underneath. Taking the burning cigarette he jauntily pops it into the hole and follows it in with his thumb, pressing it through the cloth, into the palm of his hand, it must be.

'Abra-ca-fuckin'-dabra,' he says, and releases the shirt. There's no sign of the cigarette, no burn marks on the white shirt.

Smiling gleefully, Buddy Maze holds out both fists and says, 'Abra-ca-fuckin'-one-more-time-dabra!' He claps his knuckles together and opens his hands. In the left one lies the remains of the cigarette butt.

'Magic, eh?'

He wipes it back into the ashtray and returns to his chair.

'Hey, how d'you do that?'

Outside, the man chanting changes octave, up a notch. It might be that the burn of the sun on his upturned face has increased.

Buddy begins to dress himself like a delicate parcel.

Wik is standing now, unsteadily, trapped by the low table butting up against his shins. 'So, was it because of the market fall? I resigned, now things will most likely recover, huh?'

Buddy Maze breaks into a luminous smile. His face is fresh for a man of his age because the fat stretches the skin to make it look newer; the smile smooths it further still. His voice has dropped. 'I was amazed at that. How *far* down ... But it wasn't to do with you. It was kind of inevitable, with your opting to take an actual operating stance. He can't have blamed you for that.

'Besides,' adds Buddy, 'you know, he don't care about money? Never has. That's been his great strength. He does not give a stuff about it, so risk ain't risk, not to him. He can't have blown you out for that. You did nothing but brave behaviour, really.'

Wik Slavery looks on as Buddy deftly tickles the tissue paper out from the folds of an outsize shirt. It falls open to reveal a tiger's-head motif on the front, the tiger staring hard, coming straight out of a tangle of colours.

'And it doesn't matter that much to you, either. Hell, you still got half of Sayers coming to you, bit by bit, over the next few years anyway. You don't need to worry about short-term.'

Buddy Maze slips his robe.

Wik fights for control. The alcohol's bleeding fast into his system. Someone else, now, is making a fuss outside, maybe to tell the man chanting to shut it up. There's a stripe of sunlight burning Wik's thigh. He covers it with his hand; it burns the hand. The shouting stops but the chanting goes on, more indistinct whenever traffic takes off down the road, then with returning clarity. He can smell the alcohol fumes in his nasal passages. He waits for Buddy Maze.

Pulling on the cream cotton flannels, Buddy muses idly, almost talking to himself. 'I gotta hand it to you, you gave it a try, you got out there! Keen as a fuckin' poor whore, you were. Ambelin should like you better for that, if anything.' Buddy Maze sounds admiring. Then his eyebrows pop; he carries on more seriously, 'But I'm gonna get you right back in with him.'

Eroded by failure, Wik needs this, but he recognises politeness cluttering his personality again when he asks, 'You think you can?'

'I have no doubts at all.' Buddy wheels away and takes to strolling round the room examining the various fittings as if he were in a bric-à-brac shop, ready to buy. Then he says, suddenly, 'I had a thought, Wik.' (Inside, Buddy smiles. Had *a* thought? This is *the* thought, he's been thinking about it non-stop since coming from New Orleans, he wakes himself in the night and remembers immediately, he can curse it for not leaving him alone. He's even got men working on this question.)

'I mean, we don't know what's in Ambelin's will . . .?' Buddy sounds gently puzzled, as though it's just occurred to him to worry about this. 'I suppose we kind of need to know what's in his will. Planning 'n' all.' Buddy sighs. Receiving no answer, he appears to drift off being interested in the subject before he moves back and says, again as if he's just remembered something he left out, "D'you ever *find out* if we're in his will?'

'I never heard it mentioned.'

'There's no one else to go in it.'

'No.'

'But you don't know anything about where he's leaving anything to?'

'No.'

'I heard it was made round about '75, so unless he made a new one we're not in it I guess.'

Buddy turns away and tweaks the blinds, finding the view from the window. He stands with one hand in his pocket, looking rich, relaxed. 'That guy,' he begins, conversationally, 'you know he's out there wild-mouthing away most of the day, wasting his time 'n' all, but he's got the most beautiful daughter? What's he want with God or whatever it is and all that rapping stuff when he can look at a daughter like he's got, huh?'

Buddy Maze: fat, oldish, superbly confident. He gives Wik a

quizzical look, pulling out the packet of Strokes and a silver lighter gifted by his wife, patting one free, lighting up.

His instinct being that Wik truly knows nothing of how the remains of Ambelin's estate will be dispersed after death, Buddy finds himself thinking of a movie, the one with Chaplin and the psycho: they're both staving, the psycho sees Chaplin like he's a chicken and makes a move to eat him, because that's how it is, Buddy wants to consume this Wik Slavery, he's a second helping of the gifting programme, the same size as the first. Buddy thought he was full of money, but seeing the extra there, over the last week or two he's built up a big hole of an appetite.

When he speaks it is with carefree friendliness. 'Wik, you need to relax? You're a bit stretched out.'

This kindness causes Wik problems. He can't accept. He yawns. He finds himself growing unreasonably emotional.

'C'mon, let me help you.' Buddy moves close and leans over, the tip of his cigarette pointing and glowing accusingly. His eyes swing from one side to another as he reads Wik's face.

A boyish look, then, lightens his expression. 'Hey, you know I used to read a lot of self-help stuff. Get rich quick, how to be a nice guy, all that stuff, how to remember your wife's dress size and your boss's birthday. Huh! Never did any good. Never. 'Cept for one thing. I learnt to hypnotise myself. Yeah I did!'

If Wik can accept that someone's on his side . . .

'That was the one good thing. Kind of surprising,' continues Buddy, 'a rill ordinary technique. Relaxation stuff, really. I got it off an Indian guy, all towelled up on the cover of the book as I recall.' Buddy puts his hands together under his chin in the praying position and dips his head to the side, both ways. 'You want to try?'

Any amiability coming at Wik is sufficient to break him; a cough escapes, incongruously dry and alone, accompanied not by tears or anything else, except a brief twist to his mouth and a weakening embarrassment.

'Hey,' soothes Buddy Maze, happy to double up on the sincerity, 'I mean it, this can help.' He is sticking with the conversational tone; it implies he didn't really notice or, anyway, care about Wik's momentary failure. 'You join your hands together like this.' He laces his fingers together, tugging to demonstrate the strength of the bond. 'Give it a go. Nothing like hypnotising other people, it's kinda easier than you'd think.'

Wik Slavery copies, intertwining his hands and looking down as if expecting them to move by themselves.

The room is heating up. Hours of sun beating down on the roof add up to more than the air-conditioning subtracts.

'Now close your eyes. This is rill relaxing, trust me.'

Wik obeys. Whether it works or not, this is good for him right now.

'OK, OK,' croons Buddy Maze. 'Just breathe for a while. Just breathe.'

They wait, Wik Slavery stopped in position, Buddy Maze quietly wandering about the apartment. The small toy fan in the corner searches like radar. With the heat comes increased agitation in the air: dust and noise. The traffic outside is streaming. The man's chanting has stopped.

As Buddy Maze comes back he picks up an ordinary kitchen knife, turning it over in his hand, testing its sharpness on the stroke of his thumb.

'Hypnosis is kind of a tranquilliser, you know, you can forget yourself, you can find yourself . . .'

Wik nods.

'OK,' says Buddy Maze, softly, 'keep your eyes closed.'

He adds, 'Now, this won't worry you, but you'll find you are unable to separate your hands. We just kinda wait for a minute, then you'll see that's just the way it is – your hands, they just don't wanna be apart . . . Remember I'm guidin' you through. Relax.'

Wik can hear the suck and crackle of Buddy drawing on the cigarette at close quarters. The voice coming at him reverberates.

'OK, now, try it out, see if we've got there.'

Wik's hands are glued.

'Try a little harder.'

Still stuck together – he does try. He has a sense of belonging. He's good at this, fine, he'll stay right here.

'See, ain't that the best thing? Now, this is when something happens, OK – here it is – simple as anything, you can pull your hands apart now.'

Relief floods through Wik Slavery. Humbly he agrees – one by one his fingers come loose. It is a miracle to have them back.

Buddy says, 'You have an itch on your chin.'

Immediately Wik's there, scratching.

'OK, it's gone.'

Wik stops.

'OK.' Buddy's voice is soft, alluring. 'So the next thing is, you hold out your hands.'

Wik feels his hands taken and positioned, palm upwards, resting on his knees. Then he feels a touch on either side of his head – Buddy Maze is hooked up to his temples.

'The theory goes like this, see, you have a good side and a restless side. A side that's for you, a side that's against you.'

The touch moves – down his neck, along his shoulders, down his arms.

The tickling stops on his hands. Then it lifts – nothing.

Wik hears again the cigarette being inhaled.

'A side that's for you, a side that's restless,' comes the matter-of-fact voice, 'you know which is which?'

'I don't . . .'

'That's OK, in a bit it comes, then it's real obvious, after a little while. Relax, don't worry. Let's just wait.'

A half-minute later Buddy asks, 'Feel it yet, which side is for you?'

'I don't know . . .'

'OK, let's say, you just tell me when you do.'

Buddy Maze touches Wik's right-hand palm, lightly, with a fingertip. Against the left-hand one he sets the tip of the cigarette.

Wik Slavery hisses and moves away from the sting. His lip is between his teeth.

'Somethin' telling you?'

'Yes.'

'That's the restless side, huh?'

'Must be . . .' Wik sounds confident.

'You just get that hand away from you,' Buddy Maze advises, 'you must lose that hand.'

Wik shakes his arm.

'Get rid of it.'

The sting worsens. Wik Slavery is trying to throw it off. He can smell burning.

'D'you need help?'

Wik says, sounding authoritative, 'Help . . .'

He feels a handle come into his good hand; his fingers are

122

folded on it.

Buddy's voice comes through to him ('Cut it off at the wrist'), then from further away ('There'll be no more pain, no harm done').

Wik Slavery shaves at his wrist. It's like he is roughly sharpening a stick.

Then he hears a word float in from very far off ('Christ'). He keeps going. The handle has become slippery.

He must be doing well – there's a distant laugh. The pain is slipping away.

AMBELIN FACES a steady breeze, crossing the dunes. To reach his regular sun spot is to trek over a range of mountains-in-miniature, the ups and downs hiding and then revealing by turns. The longest strands of his hair lift and point, wildly, as he crests each rim; as he drops to the bottom there's a cup of heat, calm, with silence a sudden grace disturbed only by the noise he makes.

To his right moves that solid, wet desert, the ocean, in its bowl, with its tidal slop, interminably working. In front of him, Moon is busy on the different angles of the sand, working also, by smell.

He could fold into any of the dunes and catch the sun, but he seeks a particular spot because its familiarity has bred meaning for him, its silent unchanged greeting a continual and slow reinforcement.

It's marked, his dune, by a butt of wood fast in the sand on one slope, the bolt rusting in its end telling of a previous human use. Ambelin is comfortable, quiet, in the company of this unknown relic. He uses the bolt to hang his trunks on to dry.

Having found his place and enjoyed an unconscious reunion with each feature (the wooden beam, the bolt, the clip in the horizon which allows an extra hour of sun, all part of the reward), Ambelin prepares the ground. A rolled towel for under his neck, the sand clean, even, warm. First patting his pocket to check the book of photographs is safe, he unclothes his limbs.

Facing the sun he slowly sits.

He watches Moon, whose nose is wrinkling in an investigation of the seam between the wood and the sand. Taking a feather-light crust of unidentifiable material lying to hand, Ambelin tosses it just in front of his dog. Moon's ears prick, briefly, then she looks at Ambelin, pleased.

Ambelin lays himself down, adjusting the towel roll.

He engages in a slow, horizontal dance to fit his body into the sand.

Finding stillness, he roasts, gently, on the heat from below. The sun soaks his face. Always a perfect weight of sun, here. The backs of his eyelids glow pink. He can hear Moon's pant.

TJ'S SLOT FOR the journey is sitting cramped on the shelf seat of the Cheetah, sharing with a suitcase.

Motel, motor; motel, motor. It's been slow progress because of the age of the car. And it has to be cleaned.

Appreciably closer to the Cinsaretti residence, TJ's temper has begun to fray. The open roof has lost its charm. He is boxed in and the top of his head is beaten by the heat.

He looks at Mr Cinsaretti's baldness and the wind lifting the fringe of hair and he asks, 'Mr Cinsaretti, may I call you Cueball?'

Mr Cinsaretti doesn't answer straight away. Amie gives him a look.

'Cueball?' Mr Cinsaretti strokes his pate, leaving one wrist draped over the top of the steering wheel (they're going slowly).

TJ asks, 'Is that OK?'

'Can't you call me Arthur?'

'Oh yeah, sure. Easy.'

'Thanks son. It's my name and I got used to answering to it.'

'Thing is,' says TJ after a while (the road noise humming, the signs marking them off every now and again), 'it's kind of unfriendly.'

Then his mom helps out. 'See, TJ likes to have special names for people he might be friends with,' she says, smiling at Mr Cinsaretti, extending an arm behind his shoulders, playing with the wisp of hair on the back of his neck. 'Sign of affection.'

She adds, 'He's got names for everyone.'

Mr Cinsaretti eventually lifts his free hand up into the air. He chuckles. 'OK. What the hell. Cueball to you.'

'Great. Cueball!'

And now another motel. The office, the matching sets of box-rooms, another pair of oldsters in charge.

Mr Cinsaretti is in the office booking the rooms (one each, he insists).

Waiting outside, the silence standing, it seems, TJ watches his mother's forefinger running up and down the strap of her bag.

125

After a while, he begins to marvel that she can keep doing this for so long. She will wear the strap away.

Or her finger.

When the thought occurs to him that this is a symptom of the drinker in her, precisely at that point, she stops doing it.

Then she says, seriously, 'TJ, don't call him Cueball.'

'Why not?'

'I know what you're up to.'

'I know what *you're* up to. Ma, I'd rather have the lakehouse than this. Major peeve.'

'Don't call him Cueball.'

'Maybe I won't.'

'Thank you.'

'Maybe I'll call him something else.'

'TJ . . .'

'I could call him anything. I could call him Roadblock. Or Teacup. Any old thing.'

'Don't.'

'I could call him Car Door. Dishwasher.'

'TJ, I . . .'

'No Ma, beep, fuckin' beep.'

BAKED FOR OVER an hour now, Ambelin digs his elbow in the sand and turns on his front. The day's heat has eased.

An observer from above would see his spine is kinked, with a jutting fifth vertebra and a long s-bend leading down to his hips.

He reaches for his trousers, wanting to look again at the pocket-size book of photographs. The five pictures within are of himself, dating from the 1930s.

Turning to the first, he sees an eight-year-old boy, standing stiffly for the camera, solemn, hands behind his back (of course, having to keep still). His father's faded handwriting describes it, AMBELIN'S NEW CLOTHES. Ambelin squints, eyeing close detail, trying to look past the grain of the photograph to see how he *was* at that time . . . The age of the emulsion, or perhaps the tricky, hand-cranked technology of the camera, has made the image milky, a ghost of him rather than an accurate likeness. It's when he examines, minutely, the shape and carriage of the boy's hand, that he suddenly, forcefully, recognises himself because he's looking at the same hand, some sixty years later, here, now, holding the photograph. Ambelin is stirred by grief that such a thing as age should exist.

His back dusted with gold sand, lying like a felled pole in the bottom of his landmark dune, Ambelin fans his fingers and examines his hand. His father cut and made this book with *his* hand and carried it in the same pocket as his wallet (he has to convince himself, these days, that his parents ever were alive). *Like the back of my hand* . . .

Beaten by too much sun, watching the sand cover his fingers as he presses them downwards, Ambelin feels a weepy panic at where the photographs are going to end up.

PROFESSOR SAGE TINKLER'S suite at La Paz is bare: the ashtray is the only sentimental item. She dresses the rooms in the same way as the lab: what's necessary for the job, and the best. The combat-gear wardrobe is conceived (in her eyes) as a rational rather than as a fashion thing – the mix of her slight physique, her practical nature and her ruthless curiosity prescribes a frontier image, but modern, because she is perched, smoking, on her particular look-out: medical science.

She was successfully introduced to Ambelin.

'Ambelin, Professor Sage Tinkler.'

Buddy then explained, talking cheerfully to the old man, 'Ambelin, I know you're a remarkably healthy guy considerin' what kinda fuckin' pressure you bin buckled under all these years, but there's a reason for that, ain't there? First-fuckin'-class medical whatsits, no? And I'm not goin' to let things slacken off in that department. You're attainin' the age when prevention's the fuckin' cure, 'cause you know how it is, one hormone slips – bang. One enzyme holds on too long – wham. One valve sticks – kerzazz. One more blood cell joins the clot . . . Hey, I'm too fond of you to let you go. You're the only friend I got and if you're goin' to die one day it ain't goin' to be 'til I've had my fill – you understand me?'

Then the fat man stopped, glanced at her and tugged his trousers up, both hands hauling a fistful of waistband.

He started laughing. 'Ambelin, Ambelin, your fuckin' face, priceless, priceless.'

Ambelin had smiled, lifting his brows, giving his owlish look.

'So I hired this lady,' explained Buddy, pointing a thumb in her direction. 'Or rather she agreed to come look after you. And she's some woman, a remarkable thing in her own right, this Professor Sage Tinkler.'

Buddy looked earnestly at her, his round face plump with sincerity.

'She started off with a history of scooter repair and box-cart

128

championships, but then go-gets herself a degree in medicine? No end to the good work. Moves on to free, charity healthcare for some mighty impoverished third- or hell even fourth-world Turkish peasant people, then hired to save and extend life in that extra arty whatsit clinic in Switzerland – using no fancy potions you understand, just dexterity, sheer mechanical dexterity. Workin' on rill Frankenstein-style research at the moment, maybe curing cancer and all sorts. I'm kinda funding her programme and she's agreed to keep an eye on you?'

Ambelin nodded.

'OK, so if you need her, just shout,' nodded Buddy in return.

She checks Ambelin once a day, tracking functions, down to the last amino acid. A product of medicine's new love affair with physics, she's deep into the make-up of people, beyond where her slim fingers can go, beyond eyesight, beyond even micro-surgery – so far down, she can call herself an atomic engineer.

Buddy Maze can trust her ability. Despite being banned from membership of the National Academy of Sciences, her credits won her the offer of a place on the US team of specialists engaged on the Human Genome Project, logging the hundreds of thousands of genes which encode the exact mysteries of human assembly; once this is complete it will be a dictionary of the most minute elements of physique. She turned it down, preferring her own work: she is one of a handful of people privy to the ongoing trials of a drug which she can claim partial responsibility for; as yet named only in code (DIANA), it is a synthetic analogue of deoxyribonucleic acid, that intelligent substance the discovery of which has jolted not only the field of medicine but also the Constitution, because there are ongoing legal arguments as to whether or not scientists should have a right to carry out such dangerous research, fronted by the 'falsetto screamers' – those who object most strongly to the prospect of cloning and other forms of genetic mutation. Professor Tinkler has always felt an affinity for DNA – that 'total process of life', agent of youth, the collapse of which sets an invisible, wet rust into the human body, folding it, slowing it, timing it to its set number of years alive – she likes the idea of driving down there, to the tiniest measurements where the willpower of life is most evident: why *should* haemoglobin carry oxygen? Why should twenty amino acids arrange themselves *just so*, each structure a different protein? Also, she considers herself to be fighting back for women forgotten in this field – it was down to Rosalind Franklin that the double helix was discovered by Watson and Crick, yet her contribution is ignored; Dorothy Hodgkin and Hilary Muirhead were just as crucial as Monod, yet he alone gloried in making the statement, 'I have discovered the second meaning of life.'

The fruit of this enquiry (a complete and explicit knowledge of the precise molecular sequences that encode human life), already ripening into the public domain, will mean an unbeatable score against illness and old age. Foetuses can be checked against the gene dictionary and all hereditary weaknesses stopped. Viruses won't be able to get about, secretly, as before, on the backs of genes, they will be found, cornered and taken away. Cancers will be easy – that's one in three adult deaths in the first and second worlds which will have to find various, more distant endings.

Yet all this discovery, which can sound like good news to the old and cancerous, rich enough, who might be able to last until it (soon) hits with an everyday usefulness, is not for her a reward, it's not *why* Sage Tinkler is driven. She has no will to improve the lot of people, nor does she worry the other way: unlike Knight, committing suicide over the consequences of his discovering a particular sub-atomic bounce, she, although not blind to the good and evil which will escape once she's all the way opened her box of found knowledge, sights the world as though from a telescope, with the earth an interesting fragment undergoing inevitable change – of which she happens to be an instrument. Fatalistic, she regards the future populating of this tiny cosmic island, Earth, with the super-old, hollow of youth, as an ineluctable (and interesting) progression – and OK, because she herself is getting older. She tells others that she wants nothing but to go on playing her favourite game and getting well paid for it (she calls this 'the greatest luxury').

So there's a stick as well as a carrot: from her distant standpoint (the world spinning like a toy) she can sense the emptiness of death behind her, the depth of its shadow falling on the back of her neck prompting an oily coldness. She wants no part in the outlandish nature of death, and arrogance allows her the argument that she should have special licence not to have to suffer it. Besides, she doesn't want to stop smoking two packs of Winstons a day.

Bucking the tide of self-censorship created by a worried National Academy of Sciences, paid by Buddy Maze now, she is in her favourite position: ahead in the playing of God.

LA PAZ, IN THE dark: a white shadow, a reverse print of a house ghosted out of black; the sounding of the ocean. Squares of light are patched on: people up?

Here, well beyond the middle of the night, Ambelin Sayers walks the corridors on Oceanside.

A few paces behind him comes Moon, bemused at the night-time wanderings. She is wearing a harassed, plaintive look: spending more time with Ambelin than anyone, but being forever *left out*, this is her sadness.

Moon is out of mixed breeding, but there would have been a hound somewhere along the line, she sounds like one on those rare occasions when she's left by herself for too long, and then she should be cutting a silhouette against a movie-set moon – it explains her name. She's short-sighted, in a metaphorical sense. It doesn't occur to her that people control the world; it's all there for her. If a door remains closed it's not because someone has to come along and open it, it's because she's stood staring at it for long enough. It makes her a touch over-confident.

'Hey!' says Moon. She's concentrating hard on the plastic duck. Her eyes are coal-black and, for now, focused with intent.

As Ambelin approaches, Moon readies herself for the throw and the run. This kind of active therapy is important.

She hopes Ambelin can understand.

'Hey!' she adds.

Ambelin does what he's told and picks up the plastic duck, tossing it down the corridor in an underarm throw. Moon charges after it. Soon something will happen with all this running about. The fun of it is bound to grow into something more important. So much pleasure must go somewhere, mean something. Diving on the colourful toy, she squeezes it

132

between her teeth, dropping it each time it squeaks, then pouncing with renewed vigour. Odd, how it makes that noise. Something inside; must be a secret. She'll get it eventually. She throws it for herself. She'll try anything. She must tell Ambelin what it means. Ambelin needs to know, he's always throwing the plastic duck.

Ambelin, logging his memory, is trying to be accurate – he must have verity. In all the years he's had, each is like a contract renewed, containing value he's determined not to lose: he's now thinking of his first dog. Named Rufus, he only had one eye. Ambelin's first fright came on finding him as a puppy, still only the size of a double handful, under a trailer with one paw stuck through his collar. Rufus died years later from drowning . . . about the time he started selling candies from his locker at school . . .

Still he is loping along. When he throws the toy for Moon, his breath over-blows because his heart muscles fail to co-ordinate with the valves? Sometimes he holds in air, to try and force oxygen out through the remaining fabric of his lungs. Why can't he sleep?

He thinks about breakfast. Currently he takes it by himself, he only eats lunch with Buddy and his wife, at their table. Should he eat breakfast with them too? What is tactful? He hums, gauging required levels of privacy. These are new thoughts, new worries for him.

He likes the talk of Buddy Maze, all turbulence. He remembers this, the glee on Buddy's face as he describes his favourite TV.

These corridors – so familiar, with woods carved from all over the world. But new pictures on the walls. Interesting. Fine taste, he thinks.

133

Moon's claws tick against the polished floor. A window slides by. Outside it is dark; the sand shows up, milkiness patched with shadow.

And their chess games. Ambelin wins and wins. He talks himself hoarse, explaining the play to his friend. The way the sun finds all of Buddy's face, there, the same creases as before.

Tomorrow they are to go fishing. Ambelin will be teaching Buddy how to pilot out from the harbour. He will point their boat towards the agape depths. Food and drink will be provided. Buddy Maze will make him laugh.

But will he make Buddy Maze laugh?

He comes to a halt.

Moon stops also, looks ahead sharply.

It is a fluke, the same genre of coincidence that has people hearing a particular word at the same time as seeing it, but he's sure, yes, the sound comes eerily, at this time of night, down the corridor, it *is* Buddy Maze – *laughing*.

Moon is staring, her comical ears lifted, the tips folded forwards on a soft edge. Listening.

Some distance away from the old entrepreneur and his dog, in what used to be the gallery housing Ambelin's collection of glass manuscripts, Buddy is baby-naked, standing bent at the knee like a Sumo wrestler because the defibrillator paddles are taped under his backside, the electric cables trailing. He is holding his prick with one hand, the other he has on one of the paddles.

Under the bank of lights, Professor Tinkler sits on the hydraulic bed, smoking, fully dressed.

Buddy Maze is having to lead with his second fantasy now: 'You're in the Truck Stop . . .'

She has mocked up an entranced tone for him: 'Yes . . .'

'You're on your way to the restrooms. You go in the guys

134

instead of the girls and you know you're in the guys 'cos you see the pissers . . .'

'I'm hot . . .'

'You turn round and see three truckers. They stop dead, real surprised, then they're comin' after you . . .'

'What are they wearing?'

'Dozers and dirty overalls, they're dirty as hell, lookin' mean. They ain't goin' to take no for an answer. They get a hold of you, they're pushin' you real hard up against a bowl, you're starin' right into the bowl and they're holding onto you. Dirty ol' hands tearin' at your pants, pullin' on your titties, dirty ol' come on your legs, they're takin' turns, they're spillin' into you . . .'

'OK,' calls Professor Tinkler, urgently. 'Go ahead now. Come. I wanna hear you. Come . . .'

When he's there she hits the switch for him. Buddy Maze's whole body goes into spasm.

'Lord!!'

He stands, swaying for a while, floating down to earth after what was a trip that sent him to the land of the gods, must be.

Then, he starts laughing.

Professor Tinkler is now delicately dismounting from the hydraulic bed, smiling at Buddy's mirth. (He had taken pride in showing her a magic trick; now she's shown him one.)

Back in the corridor, meanwhile, Ambelin Sayers points towards the sound. He tries to stop himself from rushing. Here he is, up at night, happy, yes, but worrying about whether he can think of anything, some funny line to make an entrance with . . .? Buddy's laugh is the same as it always was, a gurgle, separate from his voice, like a different mechanism is responsible for the noise.

Buddy Maze is recovering. 'Christ oh fuckin' Christ, you
. . . were . . . not . . . jokin'!'

Professor Tinkler calls, 'Just earning my keep.'

'This must be a twenty-foot fuckin' *come-gun* I got here now!
Looka that!' He points at the floor and moves sideways like a
crab, the strange gait necessary.

He goes through mock hell when she tears the tape off him.
It looks worse than it is – much of the skin underneath the tape
has been smeared with conductive electrode jelly. Groaning
with relief now that's over, Buddy hoists himself onto the
hydraulic bed vacated by her, grinning hugely.

For now, all Ambelin Sayers wants is to walk in and say
something that will make Buddy Maze laugh. Chasing funni-
ness: is this how everyone lives? Ambelin is not used to it. He
and Buddy, back in LA, used to have this commitment to
sensory perceptions, running amok in their own brains and
twiddling the controls, but this quest for one-liners . . . The
years of his life being straticulated, he checks down through
the layers to see if he can find, in his past, what's needed for
this – a skill, an understanding.

This is worrisome, coronary-prone behaviour. He pictures
the excretion of urinary catecholamines, what they might look
like. He consciously sacks a lungful of air, measuring the
extent to which his defence and alarm reactions are engaged.
He keeps breathing, slowly. As he walks he is counting liver
spots on the backs of his hands. The sound of voices gets
louder, but Ambelin can't yet make out what's being said.
Where . . .?

In the gallery, Buddy Maze's voice echoes. 'Hey, my
Strokes, I want my Strokes. Christ oh fuckin' Christ, the post-
coital. Fuckin' good.'

'Hardly coital. You were yards away.'

'Are you tellin' me. Shooo . . . ooot!'

Moon leading Ambelin, they're both chasing. There's two voices – coming from the gallery (as he knew it), the room which has now been transformed into a research centre for the tiny professor woman. The gallery – he remembers his theory: because La Paz is surrounded by sand, glass was what he collected. Breaking into a trot, one old, old hand holding up his pyjama pants, Ambelin Sayers dodges through a double corner . . . His route will take him out onto the balcony raised twenty feet high along the gallery's back wall, just beneath the domed roof that gives the space its acoustic power – a whisper can go anywhere. That was an idea got from some of the world's cathedrals.

Buddy Maze is saying, 'Don't tell me about it. I don't want to hear about her.'

Professor Tinkler asks, 'Why don't you get divorced?'

'Cost too much. Ain't that a turnaround? *She's* costing *me*? Gaad. I'm stuck with a wife 'bout as shapely as a wall. Joy? Who called her that, who called her Joy for Chrissake when she's about as happy as a fuckin' orphan? Menopause, of course. She's got no sex left. She's plain run out of sex. She couldn't turn on a . . . she couldn't turn on a *faucet*. Funny though, ain't it, a one-breasted woman wandering round the house . . .'

Ambelin will come up short against the rail, on tiptoe, ready for his opening . . .

Still feeling for something to say, he slows and trips onto the balcony to overhear Buddy Maze talking in an unconcerned voice, '. . . the food's great. Bladder-busting stuff. Trouble is havin' to *listen* to ancient old Ambelin *eat*.'

137

Ambelin catches that.

There's silence for a while. Buddy Maze smokes.

Buddy's voice comes again; he is talking idly, without trying. 'Helluva racket in his mouth, like some kinda mulchin' machine.'

Up on high, Ambelin begins to hurt. The possibility of saying anything is gone, the words lumped in his throat. He drops to his knees (a long way) and peers through the railings. Moon looks at him, closes her jaw in a moment of extra enquiry.

Down below Buddy Maze adds, 'And don't think he's past it yet. Sleep with the fucking horses? More 'n' likely he *fucked* with the *sleeping* horses.'

Their laughter is low-key but pleased, it breeds other, dependent laughs, self-perpetuating, sinewy also. The indoor air has night stillness so even small sounds can trip from molecule to molecule undisturbed.

This derision is for him, down on him. Ambelin receives it, an increasingly effective betrayal because the two laughs unbundle together, real, free of inhibition. Genuine.

Eventually they stop. Silence.

Unaware of being observed, Buddy is pulling back on the side of his mouth to dig in a back tooth.

The air-conditioning is dragging – yes, air. Ambelin feels the chill on his face and on the V of his open pyjamas.

Buddy mumbles, 'The guy's a fuckin' walking hormone, I tell you. No way we're goin' to have to do much to keep *him* alive.'

Disaffection trips Ambelin: a rope strung across, hope's horizon downed now.

Mud on his face. What's he done wrong?

Quietly, Ambelin gets to his feet, swaying, ashamed.

As he turns back, the corridor offers him an otherworldly quality. There's no saving warmth here. It is mercilessly rectangular and crowded by these strange new Galan murals.

He breaks into a trot, heading . . . where?

Still on Oceanside.

His heart staggers like a drunk's – too full. It turns spastic, double-hopping; the hole for his breath is suddenly too small and the act of inhaling closes it, as though the valve has been turned the wrong way.

A corner, a door . . .

Outside, now. He immediately hears that sophisticated machine, the ocean.

There's the moon, and Moon underneath it running, a blurred mark. Breathless, back to walking, his pupils dilate to allow him sight and he can watch his shadow (a perfect fit, over-long) rake the dunes.

A nerve thumps in his armpit, jogging down the left arm like a line with a fish hooked on it. His chest is full of blood that won't move. The sand dissolves at his feet, drags every step back. This, mixed with the fact that he's running again to escape, to avoid . . .

He falls.

Lying on his side, spitting sand, he thumps his chest. Twice. Hard. And cries out. Moon's nose bumps his face; she doesn't like the grit on her tongue. He pushes her away.

And again. Thump.

He breathes.

There's sand under his back; facing him the sky is empty. He has done too much wrong. What mistake was there? He must find it. The last mistake . . .

He gets back to his feet and keeps walking. He'll avoid the

driveway. Avoid the beach. He will avoid. He will head out of Duneside and keep going.

His heart kicks, finds a stuttering stroke and pace. He has a big anger turned on himself. Run. Get out from where it's stupid, here among his ruin.

It occurs to him that if he runs his heart will burst. But he doesn't want that descent into oblivion. He is too amazed. What did he do? He keeps walking. Moon follows.

Five

AMIE MOSS is fifty yards downwind of Mr Cinsaretti's immaculate white-painted home, trespassing in somebody else's front garden. There is a spookiness to witnessing her own drink problem: a respectable woman picking through the undergrowth surrounding an empty house with a stolen bottle in her bag, enough money in her purse to pay for it three times over.

The liquor is still hot from the steal and burning a hole in her conscience; she's repeating the usual excuses, but still searching for a hidden place. There – the cheap statuette will never be visited.

A wild riot of greenery.

She takes the Vladivar and inserts it – marking the place for remembering's sake – next to the plinth.

Nothing's been done until she's broken the seal and the stuff has passed her lips.

She stands up to her knees in undergrowth, while the internal fraudulence continues. It's more than recognition – these denial arguments are ludicrously familiar. She can count them off: she might suggest to herself that the alcohol is only for emergencies, or it's for medical reasons, or that a sip will test the strength of her resolve, or perhaps it's educational, even therapeutic – just a way of understanding how she used to behave . . . A little further down the road comes the last lie: it will only be a short binge, necessary to make her sick enough to give up completely.

Even her anger at the parade of self-delusive reasoning is old hat.

Darting forward from the waist, she retrieves the bottle, shaking it by the neck. She will open it and pour it on the ground.

She drags her hand to a halt when it reaches the screw-top. If she goes ahead, turns, she will drink from it.

She tests the tension of the cap, finally allowing her fingers to slip harmlessly round the knurled edge.

Neurotically now she repeats the motion; it looks like she's wiping the top clean. To break the spell she puts it back in the hide (it was never *called* that until now, she notices) and immediately begins to walk off before returning to seize the bottle and smash it like a drunk in a fight with the statuette. There is the alcohol: the plant growth is drenched with it and it's all down her right side, a wasted luxury.

She lets the broken neck of the bottle drop and feels stupid: the stealing of the drink, the trespass, the alcohol bombing of the greenery.

She can hear the jangling of the metal hoop as TJ shoots baskets two houses up . . . she indulges in a short but determined bout of self-criticism.

Having straightened up, she can see herself – a moderate, responsible-looking woman – walking up a quiet residential street, turning into a driveway where a youth is idly popping baskets.

The shoelaces on TJ's fancy sneakers are undone.

'TJ.'

'Mom.'

He's not stopping the routine attempts at goal.

'Help.'

He traps the ball under his foot and gives her a look. 'Mom, you know how *I'm* thinking.'

TJ ambles closer but she backs off towards the house because she wants to change clothes.

'TJ,' she calls.

'Uh-huh?'

'You still got my money?'

'Yeah, I still got your money.'

She continues indoors, remembering where she put her cases. They won't showdown Arthur. Somehow, she and TJ will just go.

THE OUTSKIRTS OF town: houses beaten together out of wood and tin, surrounded by earth worn bare by children's feet, by chickens and old motor cars which cut corners and pass each other without too much concern or even knowledge of what's pavement and what's someone's yard. The same cars are parked (or washed up), attendant on the houses, pointing at one private enclave after another: people's lives.

Fortuitously, Ambelin hits town walking the same street as offenders on a day-release scheme coming and going from their wired-off compound; some of them cut past looking odder than him, and this early in the day.

Ambelin's walk is steady, painful. He found one shoe a while back, which has given him a limp. He's wiping away a steady stream of tears (partly from the dust). Did he play too much chess? Did he talk while he ate? Grimly, from a great height, he wishes for Buddy Maze to be walking with him instead of just Moon (she's trotting ahead, accepting the journey).

Later on in the morning he has to wait – and he must be close by the rail-freight depot. He chooses the side streets banked up on the hill, suitable for hiding in because they're narrower, poorer.

Loitering, Ambelin sees a woman smile, enough happiness to stop him. She is sitting outside her step, holding a baby with one hand while talking, he supposes in Spanish, to an older woman, perhaps her mother? As he looks on, specifically drawn to the woman's smile, the infant squirms and rolls on its mother's knee, trying to push itself off. It begins to cry a complaint. In turning to talk sharply to the baby the mother sees Ambelin staring. Her smile has gone. She looks stonily at him.

Ambelin moves away.

The idea of a child.

It doesn't occur to him that to have or want one (beyond the natural instinct of the thing) might be a vain, self-endeared strike against mortality, a hope to be important and remembered; uninvolved, never having made a start, Ambelin's an amateur despite his age, only seeing in the whole business of childbirth a quest for intimacy.

LAWYERS COVER THE ground in New York City – anyone flicking through the commercial telephone directory will find they're one of the longer lists. At certain times of night a breed of them show up on TV to attract victims of distress, offering financial rewards for accidents.

This lawyer is corporate – one of the handlers for the Sayers account. Although he doesn't know it, he is, among all lawyers in this city, in the wrong place at the wrong time – alone, in his practice's gymnasium. It is private, with no one able to overhear his puff, but nevertheless he has MTV turned on.

He's mounted on the tricep rig: buttocks planted on the stool, a rack of weights behind him, his elbows (just a touch higher than his shoulders) resting on the pads, the arc of his arms' movement starting at his ears to push forward, away from him. He's on speed training, lifting fifty pounds (half his maximum), up to fifteen reps now. His arms burn.

For a while he doesn't notice two individuals (paid by Buddy Maze) who are watching, speculating on the way to do things.

When the lawyer sees a tic of movement in the mirror, his concentration snaps; the weights fly back and trap both hands behind his ears. Before he can scramble out, one of the two men has dropped the pin to two hundred pounds and there's no way he can stand up off the stool.

'Hey!'

'Hi.'

'What are you doing? Christ!'

'This ain't going to be a friendly visit I'm afraid.'

The lawyer's hands are jammed, he is unable to get out from the elaborate fitness contraption, with the menace behind his back. For a while there's a wild clattering of metal as he tries to rise to his feet.

The two strangers ignore the ensnared lawyer, the

shouting. Instead one looks at the machines, working out how they move, while the other turns up the MTV volume.

And finds a skipping rope. He can use that.

But it curls in the air, flaps onto his neck. He chuckles. He's no good at sport.

The lawyer has wormed one hand free but it's propped uselessly in front of his face, still locked on the elbow rest. He's cursing as if he has made a mistake, 'Christ! *Christ!*'

One of the two men dips swiftly to double-hitch the end of the skipping rope to the lawyer's ankle. Moving with purpose, he pulls the pin on the tricep rig and watches the lawyer's arms spring free.

As the lawyer comes off the stool he has to dance, one foot pulled away. It's almost in time to the music. He shouts, 'What? *What?*'

After two or three hauls, some nimble backsteps, they've got the lawyer over by the bench press.

He shouts, 'I don't know anything, he's not my client, the man is not my client. You've got the wrong guy . . .'

'I *know*,' bawls Buddy's man. then, like he's suddenly not playing any more, he drops the rope and turns away. The lawyer stands. Dread fills him. Somehow this is worse than being dragged.

'How many pounds can you bench-press?' asks the other, over the music.

The lawyer replies, 'Listen, I know who you are. I know what you want. You got the right firm, but you got the wrong *partner*. I know nothing, I know nothing of Sayers' personal dealings . . .'

'That's true,' waves the other, drowned by the MTV.

'. . . I know nothing, I am useless to you . . .'

'That's where you're wrong.'

The lawyer feels nausea. He bellows something.

The other shakes his head. 'Teach me to bench-press.'

'What . . .'

'Show me a bench press.'

'A bench press?' The lawyer looks for hidden meanings, sensing danger.

'Then I'll go.'

The lawyer makes a run for the door but it's half-hearted because he's scared and can't commit to the course of action. So they're both standing in his way.

Buddy's man mouths the words 'Show me,' and points.

The lawyer backs off. He shouts, 'You've got the wrong guy.'

'I know. So show me.'

There's a small knife in his hand.

When the lawyer is lying on his back, pushing the bar up and down the slides on a medium 150 pounds, the other man picks up a weight.

The lawyer cries out. The single word is unrecognisable.

When the additional twenty-pound disc is slotted onto the end of the bar the lawyer can only hold it, he fails to lift it past the first safety hitch. His arms shake. He curses, agonised.

Buddy Maze's man moves round to the other side and slides a ten-pound disc onto the other end. The lawyer, grunting like a pig, has to let the bar slip down.

Inch by inch it descends. The lawyer swears. Crying. Veins pop up over his face and arms. Buddy's man has to hold his ankles because he's trying to turn out of it.

The other man says loudly, right in the lawyer's ear, 'I'm not

trying to frighten *you*. I'm not after you at all. I'm . . . scaring
. . . someone else.'

When the bar is resting on the lawyer's neck he is unable to
speak or stop the bar from slowly dropping into his trachea.
His breath is cut off. The remaining strength disappears
instantly from his arms.

The MTV blares on.

AMBELIN SAYERS IS sitting with his back resting against rail-
freight car number 3072, belonging to the Western Freight
Co., at present stationary, part of a landscape. He has
wrapped around him a black overcoat which he found (it
looked like a corpse) blown against a wire fence, way back. He
has two shoes, now, but from different places. He is shaken:
the train has moved relatively slowly but for many hours.
When its passage got trammelled by combinations of open
and closed points, the sideways jarring, always unpredictable
in direction, has whipped his long spine. Despite this and
although he is wind-blown and smutty and the blood's
retreated from his fingers, it doesn't occur to him to worry for
his health. He has forgotten the perfusionist he met, standing
by as part of the professor's team, his flow-directed catheters,
his dye injections and the accompanying dilution computer.
He has instead been fixed on whatever horizon was promised
him, each new promise nearly right – as the train hauled out to
looser country, emptying of habitation, Ambelin had the
sensation of escaping from a thicket of self-blame. Now that
there is no one in view, and sight lines come from vast
distances in each direction, he is deliberately confusing his

failure by following a new line of wilfulness that's opened up: he is taken with the notion that he is an animal – old, failed, oyster eyes leaking from facing into the wind, but one of God's creatures nevertheless, with an animal's incorruptable innocence, can't he have that?

Apart from a keening (in short phrases, sporadically) from Moon, and the mechanical tick of the idling locomotive, all is quiet. One of Moon's legs trembles uncontrollably. That front paw, now just delicately touching the steel grid of the step (like she's about to dance), got caught when they scrambled up via the coupling.

He clamps his arms tighter, folding himself in the giant overcoat. His knees are so stiff he's not sure the jump down onto the gravel won't be too much. The joints might separate and his kneecaps spring off like hub-caps. But this is it. Looking around him, he can't deny it is exactly what he's been searching for.

The freight train will start moving . . .

He drops Moon (wincing for her) off the side of the step and follows, collapsing painfully on one hip. If there is a driver on this inhumanly long procession of wagons, Ambelin trusts he won't look back.

Pushing off into the country ahead of him, Moon hitching along at his heel, hoping to warm up at last, Ambelin marvels at the largeness of the sky, as though the normal roof has been flung back to reveal three times the space, unpopulated here by any winged thing, colonised only by unlikely-looking clouds, each one built or dressed to an original design, different from its fellows: some vast and domed and stately as if moving for a tall-clouds ceremony, some racing fast and sleek for the horizon, others sly and quirky – and all put there

149

(it seems to Ambelin) for him alone to witness.

The land, too, unrolls to a horizon stretched out to three times the usual circumference.

Looking behind him, the train is becoming a thin, improbably straight line penned in over the roundness of the hills (which have lifted this way by slow degrees over so many years, enough to make his own score not even a beginning).

After a while he hears, way behind, the train's four engine units, all sixteen thousand horsepower, take up the strain, and move off. Now any nuance of human sentiment, any vibration of instinct, even, from his own species, will be going away.

He slaps his shoulders, huffing. He has determination. He pauses, opens his mouth to make some sort of sound – but he can't find it.

He imagines other animals listening. They would note any cry of his: a new animal.

He lengthens his stride, watching the unsuitable shoes swing and stumble over the rough ground in front of him. From a distance the land appeared to be covered in long grass; looking down at his feet he discovers this is an illusion. The grasses are set very sparely, like an old lady's hair; he can see the topsoil is rough, offering up many stones; the flints twist his old ankles. The slip-ons aren't enough to protect the bottom of his feet.

He walks. The mountains stand like cakes, flat against the sky. Moon scours the ground a short distance ahead.

The next time he looks behind him the train has disappeared; he cannot even see the track that carried it. He and Moon are two small points of life in an apparently lifeless arena of immense scope and space; Ambelin can fling all bad thoughts away from him, lose them. Then he can join in, God's creature. He will learn to find berries, to trap animals smaller and weaker than himself. Moon will help. Moon will become a wild dog. He will become a wild man.

He's heading for the trees.

WITHIN THE SPACE of five minutes an extra thirteen million people switch on. The ads get ready to do their thing, aiming to sell off the back of this upcoming event, making good use of any spectacle, any unhappiness or any happiness: just the time it takes to sell stuff, valuable time.

Buddy Maze sits in a light so intense he can feel it burn. The roasting cans (burning two kilowatts each) infect his smell. There is a blaze of music and the applause storms on cue, lengthily, including yells and whistles.

Buddy can't afford to relax. Just when it was looking fine, when he'd doubled his gifting programme, the old man runs for a reason known only in his own mad head, and now he's found the terms of Ambelin's will and that's mad too. He looks down to see his hands doing something, like rolling a number, and they're moving too roughly – a sign of his highest state of frustration. However, with this intensity of chasing, they'll catch Ambelin Sayers, and then Sage is ready with her snip fingers, her VIP intensive care, her intelligent substances.

He is one of a panel of guests and feels a rising power in front of the three cameras. The live audience, too, is a help, allowing him to imagine the people watching even more closely at home. The thought that he, this image of him, is to be multiplied umpteen million times and bounced up and down the country and bought and packaged and sold all around the world is fantastic. It should be erotic, but he can't feel any twinge of interest (usually like a bowstring plucked in his pants), despite the fact that idly, under the cover of a long sad look, he's been scouring the audience for a woman, and has found a possible receptacle.

The all-male host, Jamino, has no smile; he walks on set worried, everyday-style, as though he's been busy investigating behind the scenes of today's stories. His grooming is immaculate, his shirt stiff. He holds up a hand to silence the audience's approbation (he's beyond that). They feel the rush of importance.

Straight into the nerveless eye of the camera, Jamino delivers his considered opinion. 'Our country is famous for its entrepreneurs. We admire them, we reward them, we like to think we breed them. We certainly watch them like crazy. Now, Ambelin Sayers walked out Tuesday, without a nickel, without a single credit card, carrying nothing. And since that time he's been officially listed as – missing.'

The music stings in: a few welcoming chords. (In between, the ads get their first whack.)

The host turns first to the woman. 'We have on our panel Mrs Jamelle Lacy, whose book, called *Missing*, charts the experiences of many different families who've had to cope with this type of, well . . . bereavement I guess you could call it . . .'

Jamelle Lacy inclines her head and nods gravely.

The host continues, 'We also have Vincent Aldabo, ex-Head of Security for Ambelin Sayers, and a guy well used to knowing the great man's whereabouts twenty-four hours a day. His being here this afternoon is something of a scoop for our show, as a matter of fact.'

Vincent Aldabo has put on his best suit. Dark with a plain white shirt.

He is a forceful guy. When he was in the Bureau he had the nickname 'Thighs' because of the way he fills his jeans to bursting point in that area. He spent his early life, it seems to him, looking for bums and non-patriots and then, in the mature section of his career pattern, he headed Sayers Security and things got better, especially money-wise, life refined itself to looking always for the same guy, and what a guy, even at the end of reckoning all love and hate for him, he was still worth ten of any other. It was more than his job was worth not to know where Ambelin was twenty-four hours a day. Vincent had keenness, he took his job seriously. Such people as he, even if they're sealing down tubs of margarine in a food factory, *try* until they're maddened, but still enjoy the slightest improvement in the skill with which they operate. Even the smallest challenge Vincent responded to with utmost professionalism. That was his charisma at stake there. The trouble is, his charisma wore thin after he lost the job, which is why, particularly, he welcomes this return to the limelight. He would always hog the TV cameras: his square face with the dark glasses and the pursed lips – it was always there, right on the Chairman's shoulder, he was always the one to carve the path when the TV guys were around but when they weren't he stayed in the warm, in the van. It's rumoured that he taped all the times he was on and now replays them over and over while sitting with those thighs well and truly splayed, cracking beer cans.

'And last but not least we have the close friend and

153

confidant of Ambelin Sayers, and the man from whose . . .
actual . . . home, he disappeared. Thank you for being with
us, Buddy Maze.'

Buddy Maze nods acceptance. He sees the red light on his
camera – they've cut in closer from the wide shot. His face will
be large on the screen, framed by his innocently curly hair. He
knows it isn't the display of emotion that will work for him but
the visible battle *not* to show anything. He takes a deep breath,
holds it, and stares at the host. He can feel the sweat break out
on his face. He's thinking, I'm sad . . .

That will be enough. Less is more.

As the host moves away Buddy catches the eye of the girl, a
member of the audience. He holds it for a while. Kind of
young, a memberette, he thinks, but still there isn't the usual
magic.

'That's my panel, ladies and gentlemen, back after this.'

The commercials are there, working away the moment the
words are out of his mouth.

America keeps watching. They clock the ads, mostly on
mute, or they graze other channels for a minute or two, but
they'll be back for this show.

Buddy Maze waits his turn. He's asked to go last: he needs
to judge the audience, to read the mood of the live programme. He will ride on his intuition, his feel for what will
work, violating the body of the public with his rogue sincerity,
rupturing their gullible hearts, his class act infecting their
opinions in order to aim them towards correct action. He
will have the nation on his side; he's thrilled by this. Seeing
the triangular shadow up the skirt of the memberette he's
picked out sitting opposite him, he should feel the push
of a celebratory erection, but – it must be worry stopping him?

154

Even as the cameras turn to the panel and the show starts up again he is trying harder, thinking of gorging himself on her.

He listens as the woman, Mrs Lacy, paints the broad picture. Along the way she mentions her book of course. A world is revealed, a network of missing children, teenagers, fathers, mothers, support groups. She has interviewed everyone, she has collected this particular form of distress. The sympathies of the studio audience are running with her. A lot of people might like her useful, caring lifestyle – and those careful shoes. Everyone wants to be on TV with something as worthy as this to have gone and done. (She mentions her book again.) How can anyone rest until all these people are back with their families?

But today it's Ambelin Sayers in particular who must be found.

Ads. Wait.

Vincent Aldabo, his hands tied together in his lap, hopes the sweat is only in his palms, that no leak of it is showing anywhere else. He admires himself, briefly.

'. . . Vincent Aldabo . . .'

'Yes. That's correct.'

The host is standing square, with his feet apart. An interrogator (he already knows the answers).

'You used to work for Ambelin Sayers?'

'Yes.' Vincent Aldabo is unflinching.

'Tell us please what your position there was.'

'I was Head of Security.'

'You were good at your job?'

'Sayin' it myself, but, I was good. I found him in '82, and in '87.'

'So can you tell us why you then *lost* your job?' The audience's interest rises a notch. Vincent lifts his chin.

'You might say because I was too good.'

'Too good?'

'Mr Sayers used to test me. Kind of go missing on purpose. Around the estate, or in the house. Or in various places. He used to get annoyed because I found him every time.'

The audience can laugh, but only a small escape – this man's serious.

'So you lost your job.'

'Uh-huh. But I'm back looking for him now.'

The host's knee is jigging in anticipation. 'So who are you working for this time?'

'Actual Commercial Interests Defense.'

'ACID?'

'Uh-huh.'

'Mr Aldabo, what interest does ACID have in finding Ambelin Sayers? Surely he's just an old guy out on the loose – there's a lot of them, running from something, or drunk, or ill.'

For a while there comes no answer from Vincent Aldabo. People can see colour rising in him. 'I guess it's his money.'

'He doesn't have any money. The gifting programme . . .'

'That's a drip feed, year by year. One hundred and thirty years. If he dies tomorrow . . . ACID have an interest in not allowing . . .'

'Yes?'

Vincent sighs heavily, like the problem belongs to him alone. 'Thing is,' he admits, 'Ambelin Sayers is more than likely playing a prank with who he's leaving his money to.'

The host is grim. He says, half questioning, 'Mr Aldabo, can you tell us what that prank is?'

'Not at present, no.'

'But you will.'

Vincent Aldabo nods. 'If it's proven beyond a rumour, ACID will tell it.'

'Now, ACID is a Federal body . . .'

'Actual Commercial Interests Defense, yes, it is. That's correct.'

'You have their authority, they've hired you . . .'

'Correct.'

'To find him . . .'

'I'll find him,' replies Vincent Aldabo. 'I've got some fair ideas right now. And if . . . well, if the rumour's true, I'd say I'll have every man, woman and child helping me.'

Jamelle Lacy interrupts, there's an argument. Then the world is watching more things it can buy.

When it's Buddy Maze's turn he remembers to speak slowly. He can use long pauses. They're effective. He will keep his hands quiet, he will maintain the power of stillness.

'Christ, I dunno what to say, Jamino, I mean he was there, then, one morning – he wasn't there.'

The memberette is looking at him.

'We went mad looking for him, of course, but he had a clear eight- to ten-hour start on us. Christ, what haven't we done to find him, you know?'

'Had there been any kind of unhappiness in the house?'

'Hell no, I bin close to that man for thirty years, I'd see anything like that.'

A tear breaks free and rolls down his cheek, him trying to stop it, seemingly anyway, by smearing it as though annoyed (he keeps trying to find his sex again, imagining thundering into the memberette without her consent, busting through pantyhose).

He spreads his hand on his heart. 'He bump-started my morale so many times, like he's a guru to me, more 'n a father, and I want him right back here, right now.' He feigns anger. 'So God please, he's a famous enough face, if you see him, let us know. His health ain't hot . . .' (He'd have her rake the top of his cock with those buck teeth, he'd have her squirm, he'd have her strapped up good . . .) 'I'm furious with him, for one rill selfish reason, what the hell 'm I goin' to do without him? What the hell will I do?' (She's drinking him in, he can see. He'd have her spanked and trussed and done and finished with. Does she know how rich he is?) 'Please,' he blurts, holding up a hand towards the camera's eye, trying to screen himself from its millions-of-miles stare. He waves the hand ineffectually and lets the control side of his performance slip a notch. 'Switch off the camera,' he says, thickly. 'No, please . . .' He's working up a big emotion in the shoulder of his jacket and of this he is sure: that the camera is closing in mercilessly, that millions are riveted, because this is what TV wants: the sight and sound of someone crying. Countless media buyers, sellers, producers, directors, presenters, cameras, crews, vans, vision mixers and transmitters are all set up and out there looking for exactly this.

When he feels Jamino's consoling hand on his shoulder he knows he's done well. He hears the presenter's soothing voice take over to move the show forward and he's satisfied with the delicacy of his performance: the gentle build-up, the spine-tingling breakdown, a disgusting, believable display.

He is so inflated, he decides there and then to take himself off and call that phone number he knows and listen to her and try to beat himself off, cure this impotence problem once and for all, even though the nearest toll phone is in the lobby (maybe he'd enjoy the added fame of having his trousers down and thrashing away with a healthy lack of concern for anyone having to look at him), and if that doesn't work he'll hunt down the memberette with the shadow in her skirt and offer her money; he will pay anything, the more the better, to get himself going again: smack her about, bury himself into her, smear himself all over her and throw her out; then a shower and food for his guts: perhaps eggs, hash browns, French toast with fancy-grade maple syrup, coffee, more coffee, cigarette and chocolate croissant and YaHoo chocolate drink and a second cigarette . . .

AMIE MOSS IS missing her goodbye to Arthur Cinsaretti: she should have done it. Guilt made her sneak off, and the drop in manners obsesses her. It is symptomatic of – what? Lifting her feet off the seat opposite her (a meaningless attempt to redress her abusing of Arthur), she thinks, I'm in a *fix*. She hears the word twice, three times, finding her way to its opposite meaning as a verb, to put things right. She needs to fix things . . . fix a drink. She imagines fiddling, getting busy over the screw-tops, the corks, the bottle opener, the ring-pulls.

TJ is still counting the dry days. She knows he's counting.

They thought about taking the Greyhound, but TJ swung some train tickets. The baggage is stacked. They're heading east. TJ has the lakehouse key in his charge.

Earlier she'd walked the corridor, flagged half a dozen times by newspapers: the headlines again for Ambelin Sayers. That old head she'd had close by, her hands wound in his hair, pulling to greet him . . . At various times over the seventeen or so years since then she'd had people follow her (like these two now, one in a suit, the other in casuals, one ahead, one behind, swapping round, never looking at her, always nearish, she guessing their provenance), and she'd had someone once give her money – she'd deduced that the stranger must have been from Sayers, knowing of her life's secret, trying to buy her off to prevent any trouble. As far as she knew the secret has never been broken to Ambelin. For herself, she's not wanted nor tried to forget him, so she didn't mind the happenings (the stranger's gift; being followed) – but the smaller reminders of him, such as these newspapers waving, touch her in a complicated way: she is irritated at the same time as being, underneath, obscurely proud. In the class of people from which she comes, a 'good catch' is what you spend your youth fishing for; the size of Ambelin and his age had shocked her mother and frightened her father, everyone had fumbled, no one knew quite why or how the thing got dropped (now she's of the opinion that she *ran*), although they'd asked.

A thought occurs to her – if she's watched, can she expect Ambelin to show? There is a rise in anxiety attached to this . . .

Stuck in her seat she thinks, Travelling backwards at a hundred miles an hour.

Mooching along the corridor, TJ inspects his fellow travellers. He catalogues them according to wealth, guessing what they carry, checking wristwatches. He wouldn't steal off a person, but it would be OK to follow someone home. He could do that . . . He's forgotten about his TV murderers, about sneakers or the length of his hair because he's into clever crime full-time now, partly out of necessity (but his mother overestimates what you can do with a stolen credit card; he couldn't book the train tickets in advance, for example).

He examines his conscience: still OK, but maybe he'll work on his justice ethic while his mother sleeps, her face slipping, the prominent mouth area covered with a swathe of hair.

When he breaks into a house, when he's on the steal – who's losing? Any of these people who are reading or going someplace, knowing of others that he's never met, all entangled, a human map . . . are they hurt by his sneaking into their houses? No, they gain, he's doing them a favour; sometimes, even, they pay him to do it so they can buy new stuff with the insurance money – and they add on the camera they lost last year and the TV they broke at Christmas. They've kept those old receipts.

So he's stealing off the insurance companies? He runs with that and finds that they charge premiums – is he stealing from all the punters who pay premiums? But they don't have to pay. Insurance is a luxury. These are all rich people having to shell out an infinitesimal amount extra because of him walking about in this long coat with the big pockets looking for gaps in the seal around people's property.

It's a redistribution of wealth. To a worthy cause. He and his mother will be needy, he's not doing it for fun (although he enjoys his work). The imaginary judge, the one he often hauls himself up in front of, might tell him to get a job, but he can't see much that he's doing wrong.

So it's a dispersing of money. You could read it as a tax on property.

He smiles.

A tax enforced by the have-nots, have-not style.

AMBELIN SAYERS WANTS out of his mind: no thinking, the doors shut. He could lose the long coat and the shoes, all clothes. He wants fur, a pelt; to be native to these woods, possessed of a clever hunting instinct, a loner with a unique cry, accompanied by a satellite dog.

Beneath his feet he can see other animal tracks – his feet impress, cover them. This is the way. He keeps going.

But then he has to stop, exhausted.

Moon comes back. Everything waits.

Leaning over his knees, he finds himself tracing the routes of veins standing proud on the backs of his hands.

Once he's drawn breath, Ambelin listens. Not a sound. It is inconceivable to him that this epic landscape, teeming with life (it must be), doesn't give up one sound.

Uncanny.

His walk marks him out: vandalising the silence. To reassure himself he imagines singers: standing (anonymous) among the trees, transfusing one of Byrd's hymns, dressed in costume – he's halted by an imagining of them in full voice, and then understands that the whole gathering and noise, the dropped fronts of white cloth, the delicate tracing of sound, would be a creaturely ritual affused with mystery, like a crows' parliament or swallows returning to Castrano; music is his call, he is of those beasts, at present creeping through the woods.

He looks down at Moon – another beast creeping through the woods.

He begins to trot again, his old body complaining and the slip-ons unsuitable, but this loping pace . . .

He is disappointed to see a noticeboard planted a little further ahead.

Making a short detour, he reads a warning that this is a bear-frequenting area. There's an outline of a bear drawn in red, with the words boldly printed: BEWARE.

The first advice is not to travel alone (he is). On no account should pets be taken beyond . . . Just below him Moon's tongue sweats; her flanks heave. The sign advises him, then, not to carry odorous foods – it occurs to him that he himself might be an odorous food. Also, he has a tin of sardines in his pocket.

He feels a flutter of panic.

After a while he carries on up the trail. Bones creaking, skin slack, the ropes of his arteries twisted and knotted with age, he mounts the path as it unwinds through the trees ahead of him. His looks are thrown on all sides equally. He stops often, suddenly startled by a tree-stump and needing to check whether it's going to move.

He attempts to call out, not wanting to say any recognisable word even, trying for a cry with a meaning, like frustration, but he can't, he fails.

Moon limps behind him, listening.

Ambelin stops; considers turning back. He stares into the thickening darkness of the trees, looking for movement. He checks ahead, up the trail, where it disappears.

Maybe he should just whistle – but that would be too tiring. If he could wear a small bell on his foot (what the sign advised) . . .

When he stops again, Moon takes the opportunity to lie down. She is trembling, touting a mournful expression.

Ambelin probes the shadowy undergrowth. He's sounding now, something like humming, but tuneless.

Water is creeping inside his shoes.

The trail hits a slant; Ambelin continues. He refuses to go

163

back into his memory track. He is here to lose that, to seek somewhere else, to find a place for himself . . .

As he cries out in his old man's voice, weak and cracked, it occurs to him that this is part of what he came for: if he has to stand off against the bears, then so be it. His voice splits high at the end. A faint echo reminds him. With the echo, the mood dies.

Moon nods along behind, depressed, lifting her ears when she hears him, loud in the silence.

The silence.

Nature is a conspiracy between the fallen and the standing trees.

Ambelin's blood thumps with frightening volume. The hard press of the sun, strong as iron when he was walking over open ground, is in his head now. His lips are seamed with painful cracks – he keeps on licking them, but with a suspicion that this is making them worse.

An animal has the right to eat another animal. He is afraid of bears; other animals are afraid of him . . .

Traversing the steep camber abutting an escarpment, he comes on a boulder blocking the trail. He stops and calls loudly, just any noise.

BEARS PROTECTING THEIR YOUNG OR DEFENDING CARCASSES ARE PARTICULARLY DANGEROUS.

He steps round the first boulder. Nothing. Only the trees listening. The path ahead twists around what he now sees is a litter of stones split by frost from the rock-face above. He stops again. His heart sticks and skips unsatisfactorily. He repeats his cry.

He looks down, waving his sore hands and squaring his shoulders.

Then he sees – that Moon's gone.

He turns a circle.

Twice.

No sign of her.

Dizziness.

He retraces his steps. No evidence. He stands still as the rock at his side and listens. He's holding his breath. Moon's disappeared.

No sound. He would hear the slightest break in the under-growth, in this stillness. The air is close, hot. Nothing moves.

Other animals are listening to him. Moon must be one of them. She can't have gone that far.

Marking the boulder where the trail disappears, he plunges into the random network of seeter saplings and other assorted bushes and hidden metamorphic rocks that hedge the steep slope above and below him. He is scouting, keeping the eye in the back of his head on that one boulder which will stop him from losing his way, while probing the more tangled recesses for Moon.

He pictures her face smiling at him and tries to force reality to match up; just by will-power he thinks he can succeed. He imagines a thrilled Moon twisting round and round at his feet, banging her rear end, smiling up at him through a dead-pleased expression. He would be merrily greeted and con-cussed by the passionate licking of the small animal. His hands would be at her neck, on her face . . .

His unpaired shoes are hopeless, turning under him, one flapping loose at the heel. Tangleburrs lift his trousers and scratch him up to his calves. The stabbing of the unsympath-etic terrain stops him but as usual he can't calm himself so he pitches himself forward, scouring new ground.

There might be snakes.

Later, still breaking through rough terrain, he does not imagine Moon's expression; instead he thinks she's injured. He might glimpse the angle of her leg (unmoving) disguised as a twisted root in the silent, slow-moving underworld of birth and decay at ground level.

He crawls, looming over from his great height, watching, watching . . .

Back on the path again he tries to straighten, but some nerve is lashed tight in his back.

He cannot stand.

He has no alternative but to rest his elbows on his knees and stay like that, gasping with pain and anger.

He's asking her to come back and save him.

'*Moon!*' It is an unashamed plea, loud as his old ribs can make it.

Six

THE RUMOUR SURROUNDING Ambelin Sayers' will was difficult to start: when Buddy Maze made the first calls he
expected the news to bounce right back at him through the DJ
wire, via Telerate, Knight-Ridder and Bloomberg all at once,
but there was a quiet; the story got stopped, some analyst
gambling on an increase in rank (and therefore salary) maybe
spiked it by heralding it as a calculated backfire intended to
have a particular effect. ACID took it seriously but they
couldn't find the rumour from the other end. It wasn't until a
TV hack scouted for the given name ('Forever') not in the US
but around the second and third worlds that this obscure
charity was discovered in Scotland.

So the legacy story suddenly grows – this wrinkle turns up;
they fill more airtime. It might be enough to deface Sayers in
the eyes of a public previously on his side whole-heartedly.

The deals have been made in the US market before the live
screening – CLN and others make money for every second the
heads talk, even the delay while the signal bounces through
space for thousands of miles adds up.

It is also one of those occasions when news teams can feel
like they're swinging the handle that the world turns on.

The press conference is carried live via satellite, with camera
crews set up and focused over the backs of print journalists

167

carrying notebooks and portable recorders. A long table with blue cloth pinned round it stands waiting for three people: a lawyer representing the Scottish Arts Council; a performance artist named Edward Mackintosh, bearded, dressed in full Scots nationalist costume; and lastly the performance artist's mother – the latter two flown from their home on the Isle of Coll, off the western shore of Scotland.

As they come in, a journo with a strong New York accent calls, 'America wants her money back . . .'

Blinking under the harsh lights, the Arts Council lawyer, the only one of the three to remain standing, faces the crowd and twitches several sheets of paper on the table in front of him.

Before beginning to read, he explains, speaking out in a formal tone, 'I've been asked by the Scottish Arts Council to clarify their position as regards the charity called "Forever".'

The audience settles.

His hand faintly trembling, the lawyer reads, 'The Scottish Arts Council takes no responsibility for any loss or damage that might accrue from any painting, any structure, or any performance that may have taken place or be about to take place as a consequence of its awards to artists or groups of artists.'

The aggressive journo calls again, 'Have you guys had any contact with Sayers, ever, in all this?'

The lawyer, following his prescribed line through the event, won't be put off. He reads loudly, 'In 1975 the Scottish Arts Council considered applications for artists' bursaries in the normal way. One of those applications was from Edward Mackintosh, a performance artist. Among others, his application was approved and he won the standard award which was at that time one thousand pounds sterling.'

There's a sudden rush of voices – some stringers, already started on their long-distance calls, inject comment.

'Mr Mackintosh,' continues the lawyer, 'having received his grant, went ahead with his concept performance, which was to conceive the charity known as "Forever". Using a window in Scots tax legislation, he set up a charity with no beneficiaries, effectively sealing the thousand-pound grant in a tax-free, protective entity which he called Forever.'

With a flourish the lawyer sits down, immediately confused by a dozen cries for Mr Mackintosh's attention.

'Mr Mackintosh, have you at any time had contact with Mr Sayers, or Sayers Corporation, or its messengers?'

The performance artist's gaze floats around the room. For some seconds he looks unwaveringly into the cameras, frowning.

'Mr Mackintosh?'

His mother cuts in so quietly from the side that it might be merely a clue to the audience as to how to get things started. 'He's not ever heard from any American gen'leman.'

'Mr Mackintosh, what sort of performance did you have in mind?'

Silence.

'Mr Mackintosh?'

'Tim?' encourages his mother.

She gives the matter-of-fact statement, 'It's his thought tha' i's a good thing, save the wurld and so on.'

'Save the world from what?'

'Tim? Go on ye. I'm sorry, I'd thought he'd talk to ye's.'

'Mr Mackintosh?'

'Can we have how it'll save the world please, Mrs Mackintosh?'

169

'It's goin' to – how did ye put it Tim? He thought 'twould *disarm* money, is how he put it.' The mother waves despondently at her son. 'I 'pologise for him being so useless today. Y'know.'

'Mrs Mackintosh, how will your son's charity disarm money?'

'The performance is that the money earns, d'you see. The interest earns interest. The interest earns interest earns interest . . . Tha's a Happening, an' it'll be happenin' on, for ever, until it sucks up the money in the wurld, which in turn . . .'

She pauses, then just adds, 'It's a perfect waste of money, that's my son's achi'vement here.'

The mother looks at her son and nods her head as if telling him it should be him talking.

'Mr Mackintosh, will you tell us if you intend to accept the legacy of Mr Ambelin Sayers?'

The mother waits, too.

Her son goes, 'Tsk.' Tense as a trapped spring, he gets up and struggles free of the blue cloth tacked round the edge of the table. Some of the press move, ready to chase him from the room.

WHATEVER NATURE IS – a system, a network, a loose arrangement arrived at through the years – it's unconcerned with Ambelin Sayers in particular. He is another victim, in trouble only as much as any animal out of its nest. The hard earth, the sky scooped out, both encompass an understanding of him, an acceptance, but do not focus on his troubles, or his regret.

The nerve untangled eventually and allowed him to stand, but after a night spent alone, through fierce cold, the bones in his body feel wrongly placed. He is shaken. He has lost a shoe. The naked foot hates the ground: the quick and dead plants spike his walk. He wishes to have other sort of feet, maybe hoofs.

At the edge of the forest he leans his bent frame against a seeter tree and looks out over the crowd of hills, hoping that a slight movement, a dot tracking across an open slope, will catch his eye.

Nothing. No Moon.

Gingerly spreading one arm, he encompasses some of the tree's girth. The life of the tree fans above him. He's under the old, light-sucking umbrella, one of millions standing here.

There's no blood in his feet or in his hands, it seems most of it is settling in his chest – apart, maybe, from that banging in his head . . . He recognises a front of cluster-headaches crowding in, edging forwards from the fringe of his consciousness. When they hit, it won't be see-through pain.

He has one life only, he's not treated it carefully enough – and broken it.

How can it be picked up, mended . . .

He's initially frightened by the sensation (inside his head) of a sudden revealing . . . profusive, deeper than the view in front of him, when he's aware of what it signifies he enjoys the flush of wonder and an accompanying thought, that this is perhaps what happens to old folk before death: their memory magically yawns open to reveal the single most important moment that ever coloured their lives – he is certain that this most valuable souvenir is real, but as a tourist seeing the grandest sight sometimes doubts its reality, so Ambelin fumbles this one memory, bewildered, but it's true, it was always there in his mind, merely invisible to him until now.

Suddenly he has his life, it seems, in his hands, whole.

He loved Amie Moss, he plain loved Amie.

Each day since then has been a sheath (gossamer-thin as it lay on him at the time) obscuring her.

As he stands, this crust is broken off him. Because his memory coincides with hers: he did forget to pay her back that bit of money, he did forget . . .

Perhaps, yes, his life can be summed up, minus on minus, by his wrongdoing and the wrong done to him, but this doesn't depress him now because here, alone, fronted by a mighty vista that can frighten him into thinking maybe he's the only man left alive, he goes beyond that and *forgiveness* stands, suddenly enormous, its religious cast comprehensible. He's weeping over the idea of forgiveness being possible for him. It is something he can have . . .

Should he go find her?

For some while he sits with his back to the tree, rubbing his toes, staring into the middle distance.

When he has the answer, he feels suddenly younger. He pushes off, he starts walking.

He is married, a good father.

He can sing Purcell.

His heart comes out of its hollow.

THE LAKEHOUSE HAS an outside set of steps climbing to a deck, with a large window space in the front wall for looking out over the water.

One man is watching the back, the other the front. TJ calls them 'goons'. They wear running shoes, jeans and cub jackets. They take with them the debris from their mealpacks but otherwise they don't bother to hide. Every two hours a Challenger Cruiser slips up the track and they're swapped for two more of the same.

TJ thinks they're after him. This is how far his fears have got: he's prepared to mark off the areas of the room visible to them and stay out of sight.

He is presently behind the glass, looking out for the front goon, who has a light-weight folding chair in the trees. He can see a knee dropping sideways out of the spread of the man's legs and an elbow hoisted, a white triangular flag showing from behind a tree.

'They'll give up,' TJ says.

His mother holds one end of the tape. She's standing by the edge of the window, facing in, wondering at her son's innocence: that he should think they're watching for him is sweet.

'They can't know much,' continues TJ. 'If they did, they could collar me, huh?'

He sidesteps, checking sightlines, wiping his long hair out of the way with his free hand. When the goon's knee disappears from view TJ drops on his haunches. 'OK.'

His mother holds her end down with a thumb. TJ walks along the tape, toe to heel, pressing the sticky side onto the lakehouse floorboards. When he finishes he's standing close to his mother.

She wants to tell him they're not chasing him. She doesn't like to see worry on his face, it's too young.

'They're ticking me off,' grumbles TJ. He pulls a fresh strip of tape. As she positions herself on the other side of the window TJ walks backwards, his forefingers running the roll.

Standing at the very back of the room, he adjusts sideways until the goon is out of sight. 'OK.'

Behind the two diagonal stripes they have safe haven, they will not be visible.

TJ hauls on the old sofa until it's over the line, then he gets busy with an application form for the Eastern Bank's Young Newcomer Account. Starting with question number one, he puts down another boy's name.

Amie grazes the job page, thinking of work, remembering a lakehouse ritual: whichever members of the family arrive, they get out the cookie-tin with men in white shirts riding penny-farthing bicycles round the side, which smells tangy and is greasy to the touch. Inside, the task-cards are worn and cracked. They show drawings of Amie, her brother, her mother and father, her uncle and half-uncle and cousins – all portrayed in action doing various chores around the lakehouse, sporting oversize heads and loopy bodies. Under each drawing is a printed command, such as CLEAN THE YARD. On the reverse of all the cards is written the word 'TASK' framed by ink curlicues. The idea is, however many people turn up at the lakehouse, share out the task-cards face down, pick up your hand and do the work.

Since this time it's just TJ and Amie, they did a straight two-way deal, but TJ cheated (his mother couldn't be expected

174

to do the gutters).

Although she likes the tradition, to Amie the task-cards are sad reminders. She knew these people, they should be waiting here. She craves a welcome from them. The cartoons used to be fun (her father had tried to alter his to make his nose smaller but they'd not allowed it and moreover punished him by drawing it larger still, so he gave up).

He would have been here for her.

There are ghosts sitting in all the chairs.

VINCENT ALDABO is stressed out, not only with running his team on and around Highway 61, but also with having to brief the three other agencies now involved apart from ACID. It's turned competitive, but he's wangled for himself the section running from Calvary up to the park. The sighting *had* been genuine, he knows, because Ambelin has a certain trick with rail freight . . . but he's late, having had to spend so much time making calls. He clamps his teeth in annoyance. Now he'll have to get men out to check all Ambelin's hides. This could mean days of running around. But he'll find him, he'll fucking . . .

He is driving back to the motel, looking forward to taking his eyes off the conveyor belt of a road showing up yellow now, under the headlights. He'll have a shower, a debrief with the team, a meal and then rest.

He sees the naked feet first, then in rapid succession the hem of a long coat, the surprising height, the arms crossed in the air, the anguished face blinded in his lights, the whole switching to darkness as he dives past. His locked tyres shriek, skewing the pick-up. Springing out, about to put

175

hands on Ambelin Sayers, he stops. Because the totem-pole figure is shambling towards him, reddened by the cast of the tail lights.

Ambelin is saying, 'Thank you, thank you . . .'

He doesn't recognise Vincent Aldabo.

He is making for the passenger door, passing behind the drifting tail of smoke put out by the pick-up's exhaust.

Aldabo stills himself, consciously. He wipes his hands down his jeans. When he takes his place on the driver's side he risks a quick glance at his old employer, who has one arm up on the dash, staring dead ahead. He looks like someone who's travelling fast, already.

Aldabo decides not to radio in. Neither will he lean across and lock the passenger door. He doesn't want to break the spell. Ambelin's in his hands.

Further down the road he senses turning: the taller man's eyes are on him. He tries not to flinch.

His hands sweat on the wheel. How dark is it in this cab? He is driving slower than usual. The hum of the engine is between the two men.

Ambelin puts his other hand up on the dash, still looking.

Aldabo steers self-consciously, aware of the scrutiny. It occurs to him to say something in a disguised voice (what accent?).

The low whine of an approaching car accelerates, its headlights flare, marking the two men, then it flashes by and the sound drops away. The beds of Ambelin's eyes are slack, giving him an exhausted look.

It happens much later, and slowly: Vincent Aldabo thinks Ambelin is reaching across to put a hand on his steering arm, so he is ready to nod acceptance of some form of thank-you,

176

but Ambelin's hand isn't there, it's veered lower, taking hold of the stalk on the steering column and twisting.

The lights go off.

Aldabo immediately brakes. His wheel hand twitches back and forth, manically insecure – he shouts, 'God!' Ambelin has broken the plastic switch arm – Aldabo hears the snap. At the same time he knows they're running off the road because the vehicle is suddenly bucking under them and the brakes now fail to have any effect. The roof of the cab comes down and whacks Aldabo. He had Ambelin's arm in his hand but now he's let go. He can see nothing.

Seconds later the pick-up stops. Everything immediately quietens, except for the tick of the stalled engine cooling. Cursing again, Aldabo tries to get out from under his belt. He's half holding his head, half scrabbling for the radio, but the mouthpiece has gone.

As IT BEGINS to get dark the lake will look like a sheet of oiled metal – dark and heavy as lead.

On the opposite shore, Amie can see the bottom paddock of the Sayers estate. The crescent of land works on her like a tidemark of his character, left for ever near . . . Further to the right floats the giant screen which obscures the Blue House.

Alcohol. At the outset of a session like this her morale is hit so hard she can feel the lines in her face deepening.

When various expressions begin to flit across her face for no accountable reason and her balance becomes precarious, she opts to carry the glass through to the bedroom. She switches the light off to avoid any chance of seeing her reflection in the mirror.

Now begins the descent into her favourite delirium. She knows the journey well. It starts with rambling thoughts about her life: old resentments chewed over again, past moments of triumph resurrected and cynically shot down, humiliations puzzled over, the want for money, but mostly the demon drink habit analysed to its last abstraction.

Then she's in bed. The room has got past spinning – it's her now, she's on her own, out of control in alcohol sickness. Whether she opens her eyes or closes them makes hardly a difference: objects have become absurdly diagrammatic and untouchable. The bed (is it beneath her or on top?) swings.

Like any sickness, it is a religious experience. Her people, her life's cast, populate down here in a different manner, displaying character in an unmoved, static form that gives them a blank purity disengaged from worldly concerns. Although they appear as adults, it seems that here she meets them as embryos or as ghosts, off to one side of life or the other. Lost love has its own special throne, arousing nothing but disappointment. Rolling and sprawling in front of Ambelin Sayers, she tries to disassemble his aura of achievement, stripping away facts, junking them in the name of luck, trying to see an ordinary man underneath, but it is impossible. His very flesh, blood and spirit seem wholly tied up with the idea of – not personal gain, but just gameplay. It is this *appetite* she found (still finds) magnetic but difficult. To be consumed by him is to be thoroughly, conclusively eaten, but that's the rub: you get chewed up. She finds hands on her face – her own probably. One eye can see out, she thinks to reality, where shadows move like speeding clouds. She is looking at a corner

178

of her body and she tries to work out which one, how far away it is. Her skirt's gone somewhere along the way. She rolls backwards (sideways as well?) and moves her hands over her face, trying to discount the roll of fat that she saw just then. A finger jags her nose, another falls in her mouth – she leaves it there. She can hear herself breathing very heavily.

Opening her eyes, she sees a man's silhouette standing at an undetermined distance away. Keeping her gaze pinned on this mysterious figure involves her in a gentle float around various axes of the room. When she sees the man transfer his weight onto one leg, lift a forefinger and touch the top lip, seeming to hitch the nose higher on the face, she feels disbelief – this gesture, even the pace and manner of its execution, is familiar to her and it brings back a particular sensation: of being opposed, of human difficulty, of fight. It's an exact replica; Ambelin did the same. A flood of sentiment comes to wash around with the other drug.

Thinking herself to be seeing ghosts she shuts her eyes, even if only to work out if they were open before. She can taste blood in her mouth from where she's bit her tongue.

A third hand, strange, divorced from hers, comes and picks away the two that cover her face. In the confusion of feeling she's embarrassed at the soggy finger slipping from her mouth.

She can smell that it is her son.

Of course, her *son*.

She has words ready, she hears them ringing cheaply in her head, 'I always . . . Now, for always . . .' but they sound different, mangled by her tongue lying in its passage, her mouth, like a drugged animal. Underneath all this she is begging TJ to forgive, but it's too much, she can only hope for

179

an academic teenage kind of understanding, due to the long talks they've had and the fact that she hides nothing from him.

He's saying, 'I'll keep you, Mom, y'hear me?'

She does, with her inner ear, feels blessed, and fights hard against the sensation of non-deserving which threatens to destroy it.

She wishes good on him. Rolling her head on the pillows, she would reach out and take up God or Fate by the lapels and insist that her son must never have a disappointment or a disaffection, not ever. When it occurs to her that she herself might be his first disappointment it hurts and she falls from grace, clumsily; she's swathed, constricted by guilt.

UP AT THE BLUE House, now, Professor Sage Tinkler is supervising machinery: hitching up the 80837 maths processor to run an artificial neural network. When Ambelin is tacked up to this, here in this white space, the neural network will teach itself his body's pain. Once it's learnt, and understands any variation in everything that moves in him (in about five seconds), it will work like infinite doctors scouting his system full-time.

Electrodes ready for behind the phrenic nerve, inducing controlled breathing of between five and nine breaths per minute.

To make life easier, she has plans to pinch his brain stem.

She's explaining to Buddy Maze, 'Like a restoration. With no more than the same attention to detail you might give, say, to any very valuable antique. Shouldn't ever be *used* again, naturally.'

180

Buddy Maze's voice floats over. 'So how long, d'you reckon?'

'Mmm?'

'How long will you be able to keep him alive, technically?'

'It's indefinite.'

THE TREES, NEW ENGLAND'S fine, diverse crop, in summer leaf, camouflage Ambelin Sayers' spindling, outstretched figure and help hold him up.

He is leaning, exhausted.

On a rise, from this point he can look down on the backs of the neat wooden lakehouses and see how they're grouped, set to take advantage of the picturesque lake, when he clears his eyes with his knuckles.

He hasn't seen Amie yet, though there are signs of life: an outside light left burning, a window open at the back.

His hope is to catch her walking on the track or on the overgrown path which circumscribes the lake.

He remembers, she used to lie with her arms pulled in, as though holding onto something.

THE TV IS SET with its back to the giant window; consequently the picture is difficult to see in the daytime, competing with the broad wash of light coming in over the lake.

Parked behind the taped line in the front room, TJ watches the search bulletins. Several channels are running them; he likes the CLN one best. They have everything on the screen at once. Maps, interviews, the lot, all in different boxes that come and go like crazy. Hungering for extra profit, they've taken lessons from the video parlours and virtual-reality freaks and from the high-rating gameshows – they know how to organise the nation's screens. In the top left-hand corner sits the amount of money given as a reward for information leading to the finding of Ambelin Sayers. It is constantly updated, including the amount of interest the money is earning as it sits in the bank (because the bank is now a sponsor of this slot). So the booty might jump a notch. To add excitement they've given it a resounding click, implying a mechanism at work moving the figures – and people can notice that the quality of the noise has improved, it sounds increasingly rich. It is a big score and anyone can phone in to add to it, winning a slim chance of seeing their name come up as a contributor with a free six-word message.

In the top right-hand corner there's the emergency telephone number: 0800–1–SEARCH, connected directly to the team HQ. Occasionally live telephone conversations can be heard, so callers queue for airtime.

There must be a team of designers in charge of maps. Some are large-scale, some small. All are marked up with pins colour-coded to show certifiable, non-certifiable and crank sightings of the missing entrepreneur.

Boxes zoom in and out of the screen with scenes already up and running. Now it's a wobbly-cam visit to a belligerent, over-hopeful storekeeper who thinks he has Ambelin Sayers in his lock-up – the police turn up in their liveried truck and find a homeless man whose only correspondence to Amberlin is that he too has lost a shoe somewhere along the way. Spare money is found for the homeless guy; the whole neighbour-

182

hood treats it as an amusing episode, suspecting the store-keeper of a deliberate publicity stunt. The storekeeper, laughing in his box, floats in the screen, diminishing, then collapses fast to a vanishing point. The background map shows up. The reward figure clicks a touch richer, the figures jump. By way of encouragement the telephone number flashes twice.

(His mom is still in the bedroom, the blinds drawn. He can hear her shift every now and again. It is like a landmark moving. He feels the power to protect her moving him.)

Then it's a woman talking, Canny Annie, famous for trapping the Wahachie murderer without moving from a plastic chair in front of a Flash Harriet computer. She's developed a homely approach: there's a mug of decaff, she mutters conversationally as she loads the hungry and bottom-less memory of the machine, sometimes even swearing in a prime-time kind of way. Various versions of the Ambelin Sayers face are superimposed one on top of the other. They have these programmes now, they're way beyond the friendly police artists with their popular drawings of villains' faces (although there's still a public demand to see sculptors recreating victims of crime). Canny Annie has scanned in a comprehensive database of all the different photographs ever taken of Ambelin Sayers in order to find mean images, a typical range of expressions. They've fed in subsequent details from the two confirmed sightings. So, the computer gives him the most likely bits and pieces of beard, the unkempt and tired pallor correct according to the number of days he's been missing (given his health, the state of his heart and lungs, the soundness of his teeth). These images bleed one into the other, long fades that slowly develop the most

183

realistic image, constantly referring back to the medical records, the photographs, the personal characteristics, the hygiene habits, the aura of the missing man. Canny Annie is confident, she's been on chat shows (the Wahachie murderer was a brute).

TJ sits and watches the images of Ambelin Sayers, his neighbour, proliferate, sinking deeper into his chair.

He and his mom together. Their neediness is a cause for him. He aims for that feeling of justice, he has a nose for it, for an animal justice rather than an administrative one.

Canny Annie moves to a full-length reconstruction, starting with the detailed, fully alive head sitting incongruously on top of a diagrammatic body. As the computer rifles its millions of bytes of Sayers data the body is modelled, alters in shape. Into the swing of her popular chatter, she gives him the long coat and the variant shoes. Then she animates the figure. Starting off, he walks with an exemplary gait. Then he's given a stoop, a limp – he shuffles on the spot in the middle of the screen.

The reward money jumps. People are joining in. TV is not just for spectators any more.

TJ sits up in his chair to make sure he is seeing correctly. Because Ambelin Sayers has walked out from behind the TV. A smaller version, less distinct, out on the track – what's he doing this side of the lake? TJ gets to his feet. Through the window that forms the north wall of the lakehouse deck he watches as his neighbour, in a representation of that state conjured up by the computer, stumbles to a halt and sits down under the trees opposite.

TJ checks: the goons are gone?

It could be transmitted by TV: sent by some form of satellite projection – the resemblance is bewitching.

He turns the volume down, tags the *off* button.

All quiet. He watches.

Rummaging in the drawer, he finds binoculars. The man leaps closer. There's no mistake. Ambelin Sayers is stopped in front of *their* house. It's a question of belief, of good luck . . .

He remembers, 0800–1–SEARCH.

Forcing the screen door, he slips out the back. Down the wooden steps, across the back lot, aiming for the marina. He's trying his pockets for coins – then remembers it's a toll-free number. He breaks into a run, feeling older.

AMBELIN SAYERS LIMPS up the outside steps of the lake-house and peers in through the glass door. Like a stray dog, nobody lets him in. Nothing stirs. He appears to be giving a salute but he's lifting his hand to shade his eyes against the reflection of the lowering sun.

The door will open inwards, he remembers. His shoulders droop in relief at the prospect of arrival.

A male voice – unfamiliar – speaks in his ear. What's it saying? He is taken by the arms.

The headaches regroup and settle in a new formation, but more vigorously now. His fingers and toes burn. His kneecaps creak, jammed solid from too much walking.

The smell of hot foliage mixed with wood recalls memories.

As Ambelin noses forward, the two men holding his arms draw him away from the door.

A sound comes to his throat, like a growl – he remembers Moon. The two men continue to pull on him. He finds he is being turned to face down the steps which he has just so laboriously climbed. He catches a whiff of aftershave. A radio crackles with self-importance. He does not recognise anyone.

On the steps he allows his legs to go limp. They will have to drag him. Canted forwards, he sees the steps pass underneath him closer than usual.

At the bottom he puts up a fight. Lacking strength and unable, anyway, to use his arms, this can only be an agitation of whichever parts of himself are free to move. They lower him to the ground carefully, pinning him like a delicate moth. There's little movement but he's hurting himself. The dried mud on the track scrapes him. He hears distant sirens. He keeps fidgeting, aware that he can't escape, but he will shame his captors. He is too old to be treated like this. He wants to reveal his big hope and shout it at them, indignant.

When the ambulance arrives the doors wave open and a team of medics catapult from the rear, fully equipped and running. Professor Tinkler exits more properly, even though she's wearing commando boots. Buddy Maze blows out of a Grandslam limo slewn all anyhow across the track and skips over in a flurry of short-breathed hops.

A crowd has followed from the other lakehouses, summoned by the sirens. They gather to watch the cameras – two of them, and the way they're carried, it looks like war. Buddy Maze's back is brilliantly overlit as he barges into the mêlée. A blue-jeaned guy shouldering a camera hops over the low fence round the front yard to find an angle, trailing another man on the end of a wire, who is also forced to jump. He's got the headphones and the dogtail mike. There's the sound of urgency.

People wait.

When the medics appear carrying a stretcher from the middle of the mess of people surrounding them, Buddy Maze is there and offers a shout. 'He's OK!' One camera is running on the old entrepreneur lying motionless under the straps. A second closes on Buddy Maze. Stationed at the back of the ambulance he has time for a quick statement: 'He's comin' home . . .' Then he's in the back of the emergency truck as it begins to roll off, the doors not closing properly because his crammed-in ass is hanging out as it takes the first curve.

Inside, Professor Tinkler is smoking a cigarette.

Buddy Maze is looking down from his position squashed up against the roof of the vehicle. He commands her, 'Now earn your fuckin' money . . .'

He's bracing himself against the throw of the speeding vehicle.

INSIDE AMBELIN SAYERS' mind the sides are wide open, the roof off, the ends gone, routes in and out whitened to be invisible. He floats.

It's where he'll always be, fully tacked up, but unknowing.

For a while he nosed around to find any edge to his enforced coma, seeking some point from which he could measure the whiteness, but he found none. Now he's stilled, lost from the epicentre of what was the whip and wind of his burst, his go at life.

Of the library of moments that he held before, he chooses nothing; instead he's inclined to invent, to conjure how it could have been, in a loose imagining.

The door will open inwards, he remembers. He will step inside. The evening sun beating through the window will have given the room a high, sour warmth. His shoulders droop in relief: he's arrived.

Perhaps, soon, he'll have his own task-card.

Is she napping?

He knows which is the bedroom door.

The smell strengthens. The darkness inside will be restful
. . . He remembers the zig-zag shape under the covers.

He has himself call her name: 'Amie?'

He tries to shake off his coat but it's been too long on him to
give up easily. With one hand still trapped in a sleeve he sits
down.

'You OK?' He might say that. He can *see* her stirring,
wakening.

He's having difficulties, full of pain and malfunction. She'll
see the veins broken over his face and in his eyes (nevertheless
there's enough virulence in him).

He has her say, dreamily, his old pet name. 'Bumble?'

Moving through the boundary of her breath, he puts a hand
on her shoulder. She lifts her head, tired, waves back the
covers. He'd tilt, drop to her horizontal.

When he is finally convolved along the snake of her body he
closes down. Into darkness. The dark, where there's peace,
and rest.

Pain races up to jump behind his eyes, different pains
competing with an Olympic sense of occasion. A TV set would
be OK – in the next room. The indistinguishable words
comfort him: people all around, he among them.

And with her, in bed. Face to neck, aimed in the same
direction. Like riding sleep together: sleep an animal moving
in darkness, moving so fast it runs and reaches itself instantly
so time stands still, given the excitement of terrific speed, but
safe.